Also by Shaun Sinclair

Forbidden: A Gangsterotica Tale
Forbidden 2: A Gangsterotica Tale
Skin Deep 1: A Gangsterotica Tale
Skin Deep 2: A Gangsterotica Tale
Blood Ties
Blood Ties 2
Sex Mogul Vol. 1
Sex Mogul Vol. 2
Sex Mogul Vol. 3
Sex Mogul Vol. 4
Sex Mogul Vol. 5
Street Rap
King Reece
Dirty Music
Beats and Blow
Damaged Goods (An Anthology)

A Gangsterotica Tale

Shaun Sinclair

This is a work of fiction. Names, characters, places, and incidents are products of the author's imagination or are used fictitiously. Any resemblance to actual events or locales or persons, living or dead, is entirely coincidental.

www.pen2penpublishing.com
Email: info@pen2penpublishing.com

ISBN: 978-0-692-51434-4 (paperback)

Printed in the U.S.A

Thank you for the love and support.

4-2-24

Skin Deep 3

PROLOGUE

Menelik

I was on T.V.

Well, not me, really. It was an actor impersonating me. Not a very good impersonation either. He was going through some of the crimes I committed while John Walsh narrated, calling me a coward from the comfy confines of America's Most Wanted headquarters.

How brave of him.

I couldn't understand how dudes in the joint loved to watch *Cops* and *America's Most Wanted.* Seemed to me they'd get enough of the police. I mean, damn, we were surrounded by them all day! Still, the two shows were must-see T.V. on the rock.

Normally, I wouldn't have been watching it. I just happened to be playing chess when I saw Trenton, New Jersey pop up on the bottom of the screen. That caught my attention, so I tuned in as John Walsh spoke of my misdeeds, tales of murder and mayhem, atop an ominous backdrop. His words made me out to be Bin Laden incarnate as he spoke about my climb to the top of the underworld, terrorizing drug dealers with medieval tactics. Then the show switched to my second-most heinous act.

Born.

The bad actor imitating me stood outside the Caravan bar with a Jansport backpack on. Impressing me, they filmed the scene at the actual building. On the screen, the actor walked inside the Caravan amidst a raucous crowd dancing to Method Man and Mary J. (They'd really done their homework.) The actor mingled with a few girls and sipped a few drinks by the bar. Then, in slow motion, he stepped on the small dance floor, rough housed the dancers out of the way, and licked two shots in the ceiling from a Glock. After the music stopped and all eyes were on him, he shouted, *"This what happens when niggas don't pay me my money!"*

He dug into the backpack and pulled several severed heads from his backpack and tossed them around the room like he was tossing gifts. The last head he extracted from the bag, he held it high in the air and kissed it. Then he dropped it on the floor and stomped on the head with a wheat-colored Timberland boot.

Behind me, I heard some of the *supposedly* hardest felons inside SCDC cringe at my glorious act. One guy who had allegedly killed three people himself looked away, shaking his head as if he wasn't deemed a savage himself.

Me? I was laughing, thinking, *where did they get this shit from?*

The Caravan scene was just the beginning of the story though. John Walsh promised they had more, more proof that would substantiate I was a monster and needed to be stopped. Right after the commercial break.

While the show was on break, guys yelled for their partners to come and watch the remainder of the show. Some real gangsta shit was on, they said. It was like a movie, they claimed.

Only, this wasn't a movie, this was my life. The highlight of my sinful past and the one deed that could put a needle in my arm. And they were chewing on it for their entertainment.

When the show returned, the rock was packed with thugs waiting to see some real gangsta shit. John Walsh teased the audience so bad I was waiting to see what else he had. I wasn't prepared for what he revealed though.

On the television, grainy footage from a dashboard cam showed me in my glory moment, popping shots at the police from my iron horse. Some real desperado shit. From this vantage point, I learned and saw things I never knew before, like how the cops screamed like bitches and begged God for mercy when I sent that lightning through their windshield. How the blood from one of the pigs burst out and sprayed the window like a piñata had been busted open and his life's essence was candy. I could hear the garbled radio transmissions as the authorities panicked and warned of shots fired. On the screen, I was relentless, more fearsome, and vicious than I ever imagined. I was sure they'd never seen the type of heat I was bringing by the way they panicked on the radio. When my other half dashed to the rescue, they all yelled, "He's getting away!!!"

The screen went black and the radios crackled, "Officer down!!! Officer down!!! We need an ambulance on Tyrell Avenue!!! I repeat, Officer down!!!"

Images slowly flashed on screen with an ominous beat in the background. There were photos of the bullet-riddled patrol car. Then photos of the slain officer. Then, stills of the spent rounds on the ground below crime scene tape. The screen went dark again and then slowly came back into focus, showing J.Y.'s religious Mazda – all holy.

Then, to my surprise, they showed an interview of J.Y. His face was blurred out, but I knew his ass anywhere. I never forgot a bitch-ass nigga!

To the camera, J.Y. said, "This guy is bad news. A real black-hearted individual. I fear for my life as long as he's free."

John Walsh rounded the video out with a gloomy declaration that the previous video was J.Y.'s final interview. To illustrate his point, they flashed photos of J.Y.s murder scene with his head detached as John Walsh explained to the audience that decapitation was my trademark.

As if all of that wasn't enough, John Walsh unloaded more bombs.

He put a symbol on the screen and enlarged it so big that you could see the clarity in the diamonds. The image was lifted from the necklace and charm around my neck that day, my calling card – our calling card. He told the people all around the world that if they found this symbol and followed it, they'd find me.

This was the same calling card my crazy-ass brother was flossing around the ATL. A card I had on numerous pictures inside my locker...

About an hour or so after *America's Most Wanted* ended and I'd flushed all the pictures of Haile rocking the chain down the toilet, I laid in my bunk in deep thought. The episode of *America's Most Wanted* conjured feelings I thought I'd eliminated. The guy on the motorcycle was someone who I thought I'd exorcized. I shed that individual for a new me, a better me, or so I thought. Yet the moment I saw myself on TV, my adrenaline fired up and surged through my veins like nitrous. The incident those clowns cheered for; I was reliving. I could still smell the gunpowder. Still hear the sirens. Still recall how my heart had beat so powerful I was afraid it would explode between my ears that day.

The suicidal thoughts I entertained that day peeked out and gave me chills just as if I was on Tyrell Avenue again. I recalled vividly how I had told myself that day to save one bullet in the gun just in case I had to put it in my brain because I refused to die in anyone's prison.

It was eerie seeing myself like that. In my mind, I was so far removed from that person. In my heart, though, I knew better. I felt alive, free even, watching myself on that tape. I loved the way I felt that day. Powerful. Omnipotent. The way the other criminals reacted to my exploits reaffirmed what I already knew, what I was trying to deny.

I was different.

I fished out the pictures and the last letter I received from Haile. He'd written me a week ago and told me his crew was at war. I could just imagine how it was going down since one of his brethren had gotten murdered. A couple of dudes on the yard had connections in ATL, a baby mother here, a dope connect there. They even knew about the war being waged in the A. They didn't know the details of it, as far as who was involved, but it seemed like the whole East coast was abuzz with the news. Atlanta being a drug hub for the Mexican cartels, the victors of the war would probably run the Southern drug trade, a crucial staple in the East coast narcotics trade. And my other half was right in the thick of things.

We were either born to be the shit or become it, I thought.

I retrieved the picture of K Mitchell and Makeda that Haile had sent me months ago from under my pillow and fingered it. If looks could kill, both would've died a thousand deaths by now. That's how many times I'd studied that photo and wished them dead. I wouldn't rest easy until Haile made good on his promise. I'd put the picture inside a wooden frame and tucked it inside my pillow on purpose, kind of like a vigil of sorts. I wanted to feel uncomfortable every time I laid on that pillow. I refused to rest easy until K Mitchell was a ghost. My brother had promised to take care of K Mitchell over a year ago. Yet, he was still here, breathing amongst the rest of us.

Right after Haile's last visit when he pledged to take care of K Mitchell, his letters ceased. I wrote letter after letter until I was tired of being ignored. I called him but his number had changed. Latreece, his girl from Trenton, informed me that they were no longer together. She said that the streets had gotten the best of him and changed him. Shit was changing all around me, yet still I remained.

***

A month after I saw myself on *America's Most Wanted*, Sophie wrote me with a surprise. I didn't even focus on the letter initially because the picture she sent with the letter threw me for a loop. It took me nearly a day to get over the shock of seeing Makeda for the first time in a year

Unlike the year-old photo of Makeda and K Mitchell, this photo was current, taken just two days prior, according to the date-stamp on the back. They appeared to be on a movie or video set. Makeda was sitting in a chair outside wearing a robe. Looked like she was between wardrobe changes, and she looked stunning!

She was obviously older and more mature, she had the look of class, the look of a satisfied woman.

When my heart calmed down enough to read the letter, I discovered she was shooting a movie called, "*Uptown*." It was supposed to be written by Makeda's sucka-ass boyfriend, the same one who should've been floating by now. Sophie knew not to send me a flick of him. She also knew what she was doing by sending the flick. She was testing me, taking temperature of my heart to see where I was at.

Over the time I had been inside, Sophie and I had grown close. Wouldn't say we were together, because my heart was stowed away in a box for the duration of my bid. But she was the closest thing I had to a girl.

Sophie held me down with money, books, and anything else I needed. She even let me get my nuts *out of pawn* in the bathroom on visitation one day. She tried to make me bust inside of her with her slick as, but I pulled out, made her swallow Ethiopia. Still, she proclaimed her love for me at every opportunity and she flew down to see me at least twice a month. I appreciated it and all, but an icebox rested where my heart used to be.

Inside the letter, Sophie relayed that Makeda would be in New York for three months, at least. She said the town was buzzing with news of her triumphant return. The early word on her acting performance was outstanding. A natural, they claimed. Things could only go up for her from there. Sophie went on and on.

Then at the end, right at the end, she dropped her brainteaser: '*Makeda keeps asking about you too.*'

Just like a bitch to throw something like that out there and leave it hanging.

I stepped out on the rock to clear my head while Mitch got himself together from his shower. No sooner than I leaned over the rail and peered down on the rock, Makeda looked right back up at me from a book.

Some youngsters were drooling over an *XXL* magazine. They were huddling over the table eye fucking the Eye Candy section, which happened to feature Makeda. She had a bikini on so tight I could see the lips of her pussy poking out from where I stood on the top rail. A flashback of how good those lips felt wrapped around my dick smacked me. I tried to look away, but I couldn't. Her plump titties bulged from the page and smacked me with the remembrance of how soft and heavy they felt in my mouth. The water she was drenched in didn't help. That's how she used to sweat when I was pounding her back out. The whole spread screamed S.E.X. She was basically fucking the camera. Knowing her, she probably came on herself during the shoot too.

Looking at the spread froze me in time like a fossil – until one of the youngsters fondled the picture. He rubbed his grimy finger right up the crease of her pussy and I lost it.

I was downstairs before I realized I'd even moved. His face was hitting my knee before I realized I even struck at him. The blood gushing from his nose catapulted me back in time and brought the beast out of me. I chopped one of his partners across the neck and he tumbled to the cement floor, wheezing, holding his neck, wondering what I would do next. My blade was tucked in my hand, ready for my next strike to draw a geyser of blood if anyone else dared challenge me. I looked around for any more heroes. Saw one of his partners back up towards the officers' station, his hands raised in surrender.

"I'm straight, Girma, man," he submitted. "I'm good. I ain't got shit to do with that."

I turned back to the table, blowing rage from my nose, and snatched up the *XXL* magazine. While everyone looked on in horror, I tore the Eye Candy spread out, and then gently placed the book back on the metal table. As I walked back upstairs to my cell, I saw someone else with the same magazine hide the book behind his back.

I smiled at him.

My point had been made.

***

I lay in bed hours after I'd roughed up the youngsters and stolen a snippet of Makeda. I'd been studying the picture since I took it. Rubbing my fingers over her smooth skin lightly, as if she could feel and respond to my caresses. I noted the subtle changes in her face, traces of her aging well. Make-up and graphics covered her face and made her look like a superstar, but I could peer right through the facade.

So many conflicting emotions competed for dominance in my mind, none of them strong enough to triumph over the other. A part of me wanted to slit her throat and taste her blood as it spilled into my hands. Another part of me wanted to split her legs open and lick her slit until it bled its sweetness into my mouth. I wracked my brain desperately trying to reconcile the illicit thoughts with the soft thoughts. I ended up confused every time.

One thing I did know. This rehabilitation thing was shaping up to be a lot more difficult than I anticipated. Every time I thought I'd tamed the beast within something would occur to make me bear my fangs. Made me wonder if change was possible for someone like me, someone who bartered blood like Pepsi did soda.

My father commodified fear, turned it into a fortune, and rode the wave to the top of the country. Then, more fearful people banished us and squashed his stronghold. Our mother, one of the sweetest women I knew, left this earth choking on her own blood. Bloodshed was a part of my existence. It dwelled inside my head as if my brain had switched places with my heart. What this society called violence, I called excitement, life even.

Was it possible for someone like me to change?

During my time inside, Mitch tried his best to help me with my transformation. He spoke of God a lot. He advised me to find peace with God to discover peace within. To me, I'd always seen God as a crutch that people clutched during hard times, so I'd never been big on abstract entities. However, I couldn't deny the universe blessed me when Mitch was put in my path.

Mitch taught me so much without appearing to teach at all. He never pushed, prodded, or forced his truths on me. Rather, he'd pose logical questions and allow me to come to the best conclusion. This helped me unearth the jewels that resided within myself.

The biggest thing Mitch reinforced in me was the need for money. He stressed the importance of it. Gaining it, keeping it, coming up with different means of attaining it. One of the funniest things he ever told me was one of the realest.

As we caught laps one day, he told me, with his pop-eyes bulging from his head, "Girma, life is like a shit sandwich: the more bread you got, the less shit you gotta eat."

After I laughed for a good five minutes at the visual (and Mitch steamed at the audacity of me to laugh at his advice) I thought about his advice. He was right with his little double entendre, literally and figuratively.

Mitch put his money where his mouth was, showing me all kinds of schemes to get money. Out of all his ventures, the one that kept coming up was arms dealing. I recalled J.L. trafficking weapons and mentioned it to Mitch one day – without too many details, of course. To my surprise, Mitch scoffed at me, called J.L.'s lucrative venture, "petty hood shit." It was during one of our many days on the track that he broke it down to me.

"Always remember something," he coached. "People will do business… um, um, hold up, not that." He gathered his thoughts into a collage, then laid them out before me. "It's better to get ten percent of a hundred things than one-hundred percent of ten things. That's what the Italians did. They had their hands in a bunch of rackets with partnerships. They paid people off everything they did, and in return, those people took care of the people they needed to take care of. Everybody ate. A black man don't want to do that. He wants all of a small pie and look where he ends up." He gestured around the rec yard. "How many Italians you see?"

He made his point, in a way. I mean, this wasn't exactly New York or New Jersey. There was no Huntington Point or Brighton Beach nearby, but I caught his drift on that, although I didn't draw the connection to that and arms dealing. The blank stare must've hung like a vacancy sign in my eye because Mitch broke it down and went into more detail.

"If you can tap into the legal arms market, we're talking international money. Big bucks! With your record, you'll have to put some people in place to make certain moves, but you'll still drown in money if you play your cards right. All you have to do is follow these two rules: One, master the knowledge of the trade. Two, don't get greedy."

I contemplated what he said. I couldn't capture the vision in my mind's eye, but Mitch was so passionate about it smoke seemed to billow from his eyes when he talked about it. I knew where there was smoke there had to be a fire. I trusted Mitch's word, so a few days after he brought the idea up, I went to him on bended knee. And he threw the game on my back and turned me into Atlas.

For the next few months, Mitch dropped gems on me like a renegade jeweler. Day and night, he taught me everything he knew, and I sucked it up like a child breastfeeding on a mother's bosom.

I was now ready to say goodbye to my past and hello to my future.

CHAPTER 1

Menelik

Sophie and I were married on a cold winter day in the middle of December on visitation. Sophie wore a peach-colored two-piece skirt suit with silver heels. Her thick, straight blond hair cascaded down her back like a modern-day Rapunzel. Her make-up was done up like she had just come from a photo shoot. Her aura was more beautiful than anything she wore though. I kinda felt inferior in her presence. Even though I was suited in a brand new SCDC uniform, creased to perfection (courtesy of the laundry) and new boots spit-shined so good a general would be proud, I still felt like a prisoner.

We didn't have to bring in a minister, after all. Turned out, Mitch was an ordained minister. (He'd taken a correspondence course while inside.) He officiated the ceremony for us while the Nigerian Lieutenant served as a witness. Of course, he was in violation of policy but who was going to write him up? He ran the shift.

Sophie and I exchanged rings and the whole nine. She gifted me a thick platinum band with ½ carat stones lining the middle. For herself, she took her own money and purchased a platinum wedding band and matching ring with a raised, four-carat rectangle stone that beamed its brilliance like a flashlight. As we said our, "I Do's," Mitch's eyes bulged from his head as if he was teasing me about my choice. Then he laughed as he pronounced us man and wife.

After the "ceremony" we ate honeybuns and drank Sprites until we were full. It wasn't ideal and I promised Sophie I'd give her a real ceremony when I got out, but she just seemed pleased to be my wife.

The following day Sophie came to visit me again. This time we discussed business.

The meeting she had in Germany with the supplier proved fruitful. He not only gave her names and numbers of distributors, he also put her up on manufacturers and wholesalers and trained her on how to secure a bid. He offered an opportunity to be her mentor in the field. She told me she played coy because he made it clear he desired more than just a business relationship. I understood her point and I appreciated her loyalty. However, after the training he gave her assisted us in gaining the contracts in North Carolina, I urged her to think twice about her decision.

With his help, Sophie was able to secure 500 ballistics vests on consignment for $50,000. She unloaded them to Black River Incorporated for $500,000 along with an open pledge to do more business in the future. After they closed the deal on the vests, Black River was interested in purchasing 500 MP-5 automatic machine pistols and a thousand Ruger P-89's – if the price was right.

Running the figures through my head, I got a hard-on at the possibilities. Sophie seemed more excited than me, which made me have that much more love for her. Here she was, overjoyed at the fact her new husband – a murderer – had found legitimate income in what ultimately amounted to selling death to someone else.

A man could never underestimate the love of woman.

Sophie toyed with her wedding ring as we ran figures and plans for our next move. As I issued instructions it was clear her mind was somewhere else. So I stopped mid-sentence and asked her what was on her mind.

She fiddled with her hands and said, "It's nothing."

I knew she was lying so I insisted, and she came out with it.

"You ever think about her?"

I knew who "her" was, but I played dumb to spare time.

"Her?"

Sophie sucked her teeth. "You know who?"

I sighed. I didn't even like for her name to pass my lips these days.

"Makeda?" I spat.

Sophie nodded. "You ever think about her?"

I looked away from her. She probably thought I was trying to avoid the question. In reality, I was looking for the sign, the same sign I was hoping to see the day before.

"Well?" Sophie persisted.

Before I could answer her, my blue shirt officer gave me the nod.

I grabbed Sophie's hand and looked around the room. "Come on," I said.

We eased over by the staff bathroom. I jiggled the door, and sure enough, it was open. I pulled Sophie by the hand and we slipped inside.

It was dark inside, but we eventually managed to decipher the layout. I sat on the toilet seat and pulled Sophie to me. Her crotch met my face at eye level. Her fat pussy was so hot I could feel the warmth seeping through her wool pants.

"Listen," I whispered into the dark as I fumbled with her pants. "You're my wife now. You're the only woman that matter to me. Understand?"

Her body rocked as she nodded, and I knew she was crying.

I managed to unzip Sophie's pants. I eased them down her wide hips and was greeted by the scent of her nectar. I already knew she wasn't wearing panties because I saw her fat camel toe the second she walked in. Her pussy popped out towards me in the dark, all wet and wanting. I played with the few silky strands of blond hair before I slipped a finger inside her hot wetness and teased her insides. I'd never eaten any woman's pussy except Makeda, but Sophie was more deserving of man-love than anyone.

I spread her fat lips with my fingers and slid my tongue between them. She gripped my head in her hands, moaned, and rocked into my mouth. I spread her lips wider and her swollen love button unfurled. I gathered it between my lips and sucked on it while I quickly flicked my tongue fast over it. Her juices spilled onto my tongue, hot and thick. I cuffed her big, soft ass and pulled her closer into me. Her silky hair tickled my nose as I buried my face deeper into her pussy and licked her to an orgasm.

"M-M-Menelik!" She gasped.

"I can't believe you're eating my pussy... sssss... feels so... gooooood!"

Her accent became thicker than what I was tasting. Outside the door, visitors cackled and carried on, oblivious to our stolen moments of pleasure. Their sounds were loud enough to drown out the echoes of our romp, so we were able to openly express the joy of our stolen moment

I found Sophie's clitoris and moaned on it. I pulled it into my mouth and hummed on it. She nearly crushed my head as she threw her head back and howled.

"I'm cummmmming!!!"

I smacked her heavy ass and hissed at her to quiet down. She closed her mouth and whimpered as I continued to tantalize her with my tongue, sucking, pulling, licking... using my tongue as a paintbrush to paint wonderful strokes of pleasure inside her center.

Sophie patted my head and whispered, "I want to feel you inside of me." She reached down and tugged at my pole tenting my SCDC pants. "Come on husband, let me feel you."

I dropped my pants to my ankles, turned her around so her back was to my chest, and then sat back down on the cold toilet. I spread her cheeks with one hand and held my hard dick with the other. She clasped her hand around mine and guided herself onto my thickness. I almost bust off as soon as her soft, velvety lips touched the head of my rod. I had to grip her waist to stop her from dripping all that goodness on me.

"What's wrong?" She asked me.

I chuckled a bit. "Feels too good."

She moaned, "Hmm... that's what I want."

Sophie moved my hand and slid her tightness all the way down on me. The warmth, the wetness, the smell... all of it gave me freedom. She rose and fell on me to a nice rhythm. Each time she came up her scent smacked me in the face, took me close to the edge. I clutched her wide ass in my hands and kneaded it as she rode me with tenderness and love. Even though we were in a bathroom inside a prison, with a couple hundred people on the other side of the door, it felt like we were making love. Her gyrations were going past my dick and penetrating my heart.

I reached around and palmed Sophie's 42DD melons. I massaged them as she slowed down and rode me with love. Her muscles contracted on me as she raised up and opened as she dropped. I don't know if it was because I was backed up or what, but I'd never had pussy this good. It felt like she was taking my virginity all over again.

I felt my nut rising. Usually I would pull out and paint her body with my essence. This time I didn't want the connection to break.

I gripped her waist and pumped one last time. I gripped her waist hard enough to crush her, pinned her so she couldn't move, then I came all up insider her, chanting her name on my lips.

***

Later that night I laid in my bunk talking to Mitch as I surfed the web on my smartphone. I traveled to our official website for A.R.M.E. and scoped out the finished product. I tried my best to make an objective observation. *Would I buy from this company?* I kept asking myself. As hard as I tried, I couldn't view it objectively. Too much pride bloomed in my chest when I viewed the page. My wife's pretty face was up there on the site; she was the face of our company, but it was my brainchild. Well, mine and Mitch's

Everything Mitch told me to do I did it and I was already $500,000 dollars richer. I couldn't fathom in a million years how he would change my life. As much as I hated being in prison, I enjoyed my time with Mitch. He was unlike any other black man I'd encountered in life. He was also the smartest man I knew. Every time he opened his mouth, a lesson passed through his big teeth.

Suddenly, something that I knew he'd love caught my eye as I surfed online.

"Hey Mitch, take a look at this?" I passed him the phone.

Mitch cracked up looking at the short porno of the plump white girl getting punished by the brotha. The scene prompted one of his many stories, just as I knew it would.

I lived vicariously through Mitch at times. I knew his Atlanta was different than the Atlanta Haile inhabited but it still made me feel as if I was a part of the Black Mecca when Mitch recounted his tales in the ATL. Mitch had a way of telling stories that captured the imagination. If he chose to commit his words to paper, he could've been a bestselling author. Hear him tell it though, he was too old for another vocation. Not to mention, it'd be two-thousand thirty-something when he got out of prison.

Mitch was busy telling me about some white chick he'd smashed in Atlanta that resembled the porno chick getting slayed on the screen when the night C.O. peeked inside the door. Mitch quickly tucked the phone under the pillow and we both waited for the C.O. to find the right key for our door. I panicked a little because at 11:35 it was more than likely a hit. Someone had more than likely put the man on me, as was the custom in these parts.

The C.O. finally managed to open the door. King Charisma Mitch hopped off the bed to greet him in his boxers.

"Hey, what's going on, officer?" He asked.

It was Officer Timmons, a white guy, but not like the other rednecks on the yard.

"Nothing much, Mitchell. I'm actually here for your roomie," he said and produced a green bag from behind his back.

I swung my legs over the bed, preparing a diversion so Mitch could tuck the phone while I packed for lock-up.

"What's up, Timmons? What am I accused of now?" I joked.

Officer Timmons smiled. "Nothing this time," he claimed.

"What's the bag for then?"

"Good news," Officer Timmons chimed. "You're transferring tomorrow."

"Transferring? To where?"

He smiled. "To Columbia. Stevenson."

CHAPTER 2

Makeda

I was lying in bed half-asleep when Haile snuck in the bedroom with a duffel bag flung over his shoulder. This was the second bag in as many days. The last one was filled to the rim with money. He didn't offer me an explanation and I didn't ask for one. However, I had to inquire about this one. I mean Christmas was just a few days away, but Haile didn't resemble the Santa Claus I remembered and unless he was doling out gifts to the hood, this was a problem.

I had a lot going for me at this time. I had to fly to New York and Cali to do press for the upcoming movie release. Even though it was only being released in select theaters, it was still overall a good opportunity for me. Seeing as how Tiffany was cased up, I didn't intend to follow in her footsteps.

I waited for Haile to put the bag in the closet, then I snuck up behind him, snapped the lights on, and froze.

Haile's gloves were covered in blood.

"Makeda!" He barked. "What the fuck are you doing?!"

My words got lost in my throat. Upon seeing all the blood, I caught a flashback of New Jersey.

"W-what are you doing?" I managed to spill out.

His look was a stern rebuke. "Business."

"What's in the bag?"

He sighed deeply. "Baby, go back to bed. You don't want to know what's in the bag, trust me."

What could I do? It's not like me pressing him was going to change anything. What was done was done. Nothing I said could erase the blood on his hands. So, I lumbered back to bed and watched with one eye open as he extracted thick bundles of bills and stuffed them into the safe.

I noticed he left something in the bag, so when he went to shower, I tip-toed out of the bed to inspect it. The bag sat lopsided in the closet, still weighed down by its mysterious contents. I touched the round bulge at the bottom. Felt like a basketball. I pushed into the bag with two fingers and they came back wet and sticky. I waited a moment then pulled the duffle bag open at the top. Just as I was about to peek inside, the bathroom door was snatched open.

I stumbled back into the closet and froze. With abated breath, I watched Haile as he stumbled out of the bathroom, naked and wet, his dick swinging.

"Makeda!" He yelled, searching the room for me. "Where you at? Got this fuckin' soap in my eye and it's not even any more in there." He grumbled. "Makeda!"

As I watched him move it was obvious he couldn't see me. Guess he was blinded by the soap.

I seized the moment and crawled past him, climbed into the bed, and pulled the covers up to my neck.

"Huh?" I called out to him lightly, as if I had been asleep.

Haile stumbled into the bed. "Shit! Stumped my fuckin toe!" He hissed. "Makeda! Help me get this shit out my eye."

I grabbed the satin sheet, pulled a small corner, and wiped the soap from his eyes. As soon as he opened them, I kissed him.

"What's that for?"

I shrugged. "Just because."

"Your ass!"

I laughed. "Okay, you got me," I admitted. "It's a small apology for earlier. I was wrong for minding your business."

He smirked, then turned around. "You damn right you were." He rummaged through the bathroom cabinets. "Where's the soap?"

I flipped on the light to help him. As I stepped onto the thick white carpet I looked toward the closet and saw a trail of dots leading from the closet. Upon close inspection I realized it was the impressions I left when I snuck from the closet. They looked like dollar coins of blood.

I quickly grabbed the soap and led Haile back into the bathroom.

"Makeda, what are you doing?" Haile barked.

I grabbed his dick. “I’m doing this, but that’s for later.”

I took my time washing him while he zoned out, probably recalling whatever he did to get that bag full of money.

He’d told me he was done killing. He only picked up Slim’s money for him, just to keep a presence in the streets. Most of the time he was out he hung around inside the studio with Dirty Red overseeing his album, which was due to be released in a couple of months. Dirty Red had already dropped a mixtape titled, “Free Lil Slim” that was taking the streets by storm. You couldn’t go anywhere in Atlanta and not see at least ten people rocking that shirt.

For the most part Haile appeared to be keeping his word. Until now. There was no denying his history though, and one plus one equaled two. Judging from his bloody hands, he had killed again.

I soaped the sponge up good and washed his back. “So, you’re not coming back to New York with me for the premiere?” I asked him.

He shook his head and water from the ends of his long braids slapped me in the face. “Can’t babe. I still got some business down here to handle. When you say you leave again?”

“The day after Christmas.” I replied, purposely sounding dejected. “They want me to do some radio and television, mostly tri-state stuff.

He nodded. “You gonna see your mother while you’re up there?”

"Yeah. Remember? That's why I'm leaving early, so I can spend Christmas with her."

"Early? When did we decide on that?"

"Remember sweetie we... never mind, forget it." I sucked my teeth. "Told you, you don't listen to me no more."

I tried to exit the shower, but he pulled me back. "Wait Keda!" He pulled me to him and hugged me. Just being so close to him felt so good and the scent of his Black soap was refreshing. "I'm sorry. Okay? I'm sorry. I've just been going through so much lately with all this shit in the streets. Got Slim's trial coming up. I gotta make sure I tie up the loose ends on that. Then Red's album coming up. Plus, these new niggas out here just won't let up." He sighed deeply and palmed his forehead.

"At the top of the year, I'll make it up to you. We will go away to an island somewhere and just chill. Me and you just chilling in the sun. How about Cape Verde?" He pulled me into him and kissed me deeply on my lips. "Huh? You like that? Just me and you off the coast of our homeland?"

This is what I loved about him. He was so sweet at times, nothing like what his enemies saw of him. As hard and violent as he could be, he could be equally as soft and sweet.

"Sounds good." I replied dryly.

After we exited the shower, Haile carried me to the bed in his powerful arms. He laid me down and made sweet love to me. Each touch was like small bombs going off beneath my skin. He was patient and strong, demanding and accommodating, like he was trying extra hard to please me.

Afterwards, we lay inside each other's arms, spent, and satisfied, listening to Jagged Edge. Rain had begun to fall outside our huge glass balcony. Thick drops accompanied by booming lightning that shook the sky and lit up the night. An eerie feeling chilled me as if the thunder and rain was a prelude of things to come.

Out of the blue, Haile pulled me to him and asked, "When is the last time you spoke to Tiffany?"

I thought the question was odd, however come to think of it, I hadn't spoken to her in a while.

"It's been a while," I replied as I turned to face him. "Why?"

He was slow to answer. He stared at the balcony where the rain fell. "That's your girl and all, I respect your bond. But..."

"But what?" My heart started thumping as I inferred what he was insinuating. "But what Haile?"

Haile was silent. Then he just sighed and came out with it. "I received word from my lawyer." He paused a moment before he hurled a dagger in my chest. "She's talking, babe. Simple as that."

My heart dropped. I knew what that meant. There were rules to the game, and the game was the game. No matter if it was Haile, Slim, me, or Tiffany. If what he said was true, then Tiffany had crossed the code. I cursed her and myself for getting involved in this life. No matter the prestige, money, fame... it all ended the same way. But did it have to?

"So, that's it, huh?" I asked Haile. "You gotta take her out? Kill her? I thought you were done with the killing?" I reminded him.

"First of all, I'll always do *whatever* it takes for my team to win." He assured me. "But it's not up to me if Tiffany lives or not. It's up to her." He shrugged. "I mean, she knows what the rules are; she's been around. She knows there are consequences for crossing the code. She should be straight though. She's already proved that she'd do whatever it takes to live life free."

I sighed with relief. "Thank you."

He smirked, even in the dim light I could tell he was grinning. "Don't thank me. Thank her," he said.

***

Two days later Haile took me to Hartsfield Jackson Airport and waited with me until my departure time. He had been extra nice to me for the past week and this day was no different. We laughed and joked like old times, as if we weren't at war, although I saw his eyes scanning the expansive crowds constantly. His head was on a swivel beneath his dark blue Polo baseball cap.

Haile dug inside his True Religion jean pockets to retrieve more money to give me for my trip. As he peeled off bills in his pocket, my phone rang with a government number.

It was Tiffany.

I was excited to hear from my friend. I hadn't spoken with her in a while, so I rushed to accept the call.

"Tiffany? Heeeeey girl!" There was sobbing on the other end of the phone. "Tiffany?"

"How could you let them do this to me?" Tiffany whispered. "How? I told you to tell them I was gonna be strong."

"Tiff, what are you talking about?"

"You know! You know what I'm talking about!"

"Tiffany, calm down. I promise you; I have no idea what you're talking about."

She issued a wicked chuckle, like she was breaking down. "Well, ask him then. Ask him what he did with my family, because they're missing – and they're always home for Christmas. *Ask him*!!!"

"Ask who?" I replied, glancing at Haile out the corner of my eyes. He was dialed into my conversation so hard I might as well have been on speaker phone. I mouthed the word, *Tiffany* to let him know who I was on the phone with.

Immediately, he signaled for me to end the call, which I thought was weird. He was damn near hysterical. His mood forced Tiffany's words to echo in my head. Things were becoming clearer now.

On the phone Tiffany said, "You know who I'm talking about!"

"No, I don't! Talk to me, Tiff."

She chuckled a sad attempt at humor. "Aiight then, you don't know. Just tell them... tell them... I ain't gonna say nothing. Please? Tell 'em just don't hurt my family. Please?" She broke down crying. "Please?!"

I closed my eyes and grimaced. "I got you, Tiffany." I promised. "Whatever you want. I'll make— "

My promise was cut off when Haile snatched the phone from my hand and smashed it into the ground. He stomped on it with his black boots a couple of times for extra measure.

"What did you do that for?!" I asked, looking at my broken phone.

"Don't talk to her no more. Okay. She's *hot* and not to be trusted. Forget about her."

I narrowed my eyes into inquisitive slits. "What did you do?" I asked. He ignored me. "Haile? What did you do?"

He averted my gaze. "I did what had to be done," he replied vaguely.

A sinking feeling pierced my gut as I imagined him doing what had to be done to my friend's family. I knew Haile was a monster in human clothing and I could just imagine the worst.

They announced my flight and I looked at Haile with disgust. I shook my head at him. "I can't believe you."

He swallowed the lump in his throat. "You better, and she better believe it too." He pulled me to him for a kiss. "While you up there, make sure you drop in to see Slim. Tell him everything should be okay now."

I had no idea what he was referring to, but I knew it could only be bad for anybody opposing the gang.

Little did I know, it would be one of the most gruesome acts in the long, bloody history in the bond between the S.K.G and O.A.U.

CHAPTER 3

Menelik

The New Year came in and I couldn't have been happier. This was my year, my final calendar. Even though I was at a pre-school of a prison, I still wouldn't allow it to dim my shine.

Stevenson "Corruptional" Institution was a Level 1 minimum-security facility located in Columbia, South Carolina, just off Broad River Road. The road should've been called Prison River Road because there were no less than seven prisons on the road, not to mention the SCDC headquarters and the headquarters for the State Law Enforcement Division, better known as SLED. Broad River Road was the nucleus of the operations that kept Black miscreants in their place in South Carolina. Just up the street from my prison was the spot Makeda did her time, a low-level women's facility named Goodman. I could damn near see her prison from the back of the rec field on my yard.

I really couldn't call Stevenson a prison. There were no razor wires surrounding the joint, only a six-foot chain link fence that probably served more to keep the herd of cattle grazing in the surrounding grass from coming in than us going out. The whole yard was about half the size of my previous institution, Perry's recreation field. A gazebo sat in the middle of the yard, a full-court basketball and handball court was at the back of the yard near the pull-up and dip bars. All types of shade trees covered the yard and at the back was another part of the yard reserved for "Shock" inmates.

Shock inmates were youth offenders on their first strike. They participated in a 90-day boot camp to clear their records. We were off limits to them, but they damn sure crowded our space every morning at, like, the crack of dawn marching and drilling with those loud-ass cadences. Even though it was aggravating as hell, I could deal with it.

What I caught hell coping with was the living arrangements.

At all my previous joints I was behind a door, meaning my cell had a door I could close and retreat from the madness of prison. I could kinda get a little privacy behind the door. Stevenson was the complete opposite. Stevenson had an open-ward setup where prisoners lived side by side and, in some cases, on top of each other. I'm talking three feet away. And all these dudes were on some real ignorant shit, so I had to listen to these fools argue all day about people they knew nothing about. Shit like who had the most money, Jay-Z or Puffy? Who Melyssa Ford was fucking? Which rapper was still selling dope? All this bullshit! All conversations that didn't change their existence one way or the other. Call me institutionalized, but I longed for a door to block me off from this type of blissful ignorance.

As if that couldn't get worse, the rules of the institution were super-strict. At Perry and even Kershaw, the routine was sleeping all day and stay up all night. It seemed to help the time speed by. At Stevenson, you had to be up promptly at 7:30 a.m. and couldn't lay back down until after 4 p.m.

Rules were one thing; all institutions had them. However, having rules and enforcing them were two different things. At Stevenson, they enforced these rules!

Every fifteen minutes, an officer walked around to check and make sure inmates weren't sleeping. Hell, even if you could sneak a wink of shut eye in, it would be short-lived. They counted every two hours! Standing counts. That shit grew tired real fast. I was ready to spazz out on somebody just to go back behind a fence and finish my bid. However, Stevenson did have its advantages.

Because the yard was so small and wide open, we could get anything in. Phones, drugs, DVD players, MP3's, whatever, and visitation was pornographic! It went down in the Visitation room with more women on their knees on Sunday morning than inside the chapel. Stevenson also offered jobs that allowed inmates to go on the street and work. After being confined to institutions for years, being close to the real world was welcomed. Even though I wasn't ready for that, the option was always good to have. My style was getting other inmates to put work in for me.

Since a lot of other prisoners were broke compared to my commissary, I kind of took a few of them in as surrogates, giving them canteen and letting them cook for us. A couple of dudes had heard of my exploits behind the fences and quietly spread the word that, despite my pretty boy looks, I did get busy. Using my young network of sycophants, I scored another Smart Phone (I'd left the other one with Mitch) and an MP3 player uploaded with Dirty Red's hits, as well as a few other acts I was checking for. Once I learned the routine of the yard, I settled into a nice little rhythm to finish out my stretch.

My mornings were spent perusing all my newspapers. In the afternoons, I made sure the young dudes cooked a feast for us. In the evenings I damaged the earth with push-ups and tried to tear the pull-up and dip bars from the ground. At night, I talked to Sophie or surfed the web for contracts or just miscellaneous shit.

One morning, a couple of days after Christmas, I opened the Atlanta-Journal Constitution and the headline punched me in the gut. It read:

DRUG WAR CLAIMS CHILD
IN NIMROD MURDERS!

I knew if drugs and violence were involved in Atlanta, Haile was someone present in the details.

I read the article and in the second line my hunch was confirmed. The SKG was allegedly behind the murders. The victims were the aunt, cousin and fiancée of Lil' Slim's girlfriend, the model chick, Tiffany Gauge.

According to the paper the Feds moved Tiffany down South after she agreed to testify against Lil' Slim in exchange for immunity. The murders were committed to silence her testimony, the authorities claimed. Even though I knew they were probably right, I found it hard to believe Haile was behind the gruesome acts. They were just too barbaric, too much for even our black hearts.

The media dubbed them the 'Nimrod Murders' because all three victims were killed and beheaded. Then, in a nod to the mythological Nimrod, all the heads were hung on the Christmas tree in the living room like ornaments. The 8-year-old boy's head was placed at the top of the tree where a star should've been. The killing was an ode to the origin of the Christmas ritual, which derived from Nimrod's death.

Authorities were alerted to the house after the neighbors reported a foul odor emanating from the home. This, after the aunt was reported missing. At the time of the article, her body was yet to be discovered, but her head dangled from the Christmas tree in her living room as a warning disguised in the form of a present.

As soon as I finished reading the article, I texted Haile, but he never responded. That had been occurring a lot lately. He had gone ghost on me. He stopped returning my calls and text and I feared the worst. Surely, it would only be a matter of time before his fast life caught up with him.

***

On January 25, one of my sycophants rushed inside my cube all excited and told me I had a visit. He was super-geeked about the car he'd seen in the parking lot that the person who had come to visit me had rode in. It was an Aston Martin Vanquish, the color of dandruff. (Because the yard was a Level 1, the parking lot was right in front of the building and able to be seen from most of the dorms.) He said he saw a "bad White bitch" stepping out the car that favored a tall version of the rapper Ice T's wife, Coco. I wanted to school him that most Germans hate to be called White, since White was a term associated with the Afrikaners that fled to South Africa from Germany and was once associated with Hitler, but I didn't waste my time. To most American Blacks, white skin equaled White. Period.

I strolled into the classroom that doubled as a visitation room, eager to see my wife. What started out as a relationship of convenience was turning into more. As Sophie stood to hug me, I felt my heart skip a beat.

"Her baby! I missed you!" She whispered into my ear as she rested her head on my shoulder. She felt so good in my arms.

"I missed you too," I replied. This time I really meant it, which surprised me.

"Did you really?"

"Yeah, I did," I admitted.

"Aww."

We settled down at a small table. There were about fifteen other dudes on visit, about 10% of the yard. All of them were looking at us on the sly.

"I have three surprises for you," Sophie teased. "You want to guess?"

"You know I can't figure out the mind of a woman."

We both laughed.

"Okay," she said, and ticked off her fingers. "One, I bought us a place in Charlotte, North Carolina, and I'm looking for office space for the company."

"Why Charlotte?"

"I knew you'd ask," she smiled. "Number one, Charlotte is only an hour from here so I can see you more. Two, it has an international airport for us to receive our shipments. Three, it's in state with a company we're doing a lot of business with so we can save on taxes and shipping. Four, it's one of the fastest growing cities in the South, so it's a great place to raise kids."

"Kids? You want kids?" I asked.

She stared at me with a blank look, waiting on me to read her mind. Then it hit me.

"Wait... kids... ummmm... you need to tell me something?"

She gave me a plastic smile. "Surprise!"

I knew what I thought she was saying but I had to be clear. "Wait. You're pregnant?"

"Yep. Just found out Friday."

"Wow…umm…wow!"

"Isn't that great?!"

I thought about Makeda and the twins we lost. A tinge of regret singed my brain—just for a second.

"Yeah, that's great, babe."

"You don't sound too happy."

"Oh no, no, trust me, I am," I stated. "It's just, I want to be home when the baby's born, you know. This being my first child and all."

She waved her hand. "Don't worry about that; I'm just happy to have a version of you all to myself. Ooh, wait," she said as if she forgot something. "I have one more surprise for you."

"Another one?"

"Yes! Come on!"

Sophie led me outside by the vending machines within sight of the parking lot. She pointed to the white Aston Martin with the chrome honeycomb style rims.

"See that over there?" She said, beaming. "That's yours. Happy New Year!"

I was speechless. My wife had bought me a quarter-million-dollar exotic car. It was beautiful but –

"Don't worry. I bought it with my own money," she interjected, reading my mind.

I giggled, exhaled, and then admired the glint of the cream paint beneath the sunlight. The rims were shining so hard it was like they were winking at me. I could see the snow-white interior through the lightly tinted windows.

Sophie pulled me to her and burrowed her gaze into mine. “I love you with all my heart, Menelik.” She kissed me and slipped her tongue inside my mouth.

While I kissed her back, I kept thinking, *Damn, I’ma be a daddy…*

Later that night after Sophie left, I surfed the web searching for something to latch my thoughts onto when I stumbled upon a site that claimed to have Makeda’s name beside a video of a sex tape. I thought it was a fake. A lot of companies used legitimate models’ images to hawk their wares. Some models were even in on it and profited on the back end from the use of the photos.

I clicked on the video and damn near lost my mind.

CHAPTER 4

Makeda

The movie was better than everyone anticipated. Everyone at the premiere seemed to really enjoy themselves. Because I was the star of the movie, I receive royal treatment, just like back in the days. Critics were calling me the Female Phoenix, after the mythological creature that rose from its own ashes.

In the final edit, K Mitchell had doubled my screen time. It was as if he really believed I was a star. Even from the grave he was still promoting me. Good thing I spoke so highly of him in my pre-viewing speech.

At the conclusion of the movie, I posed to take pictures for the press and did a few more interviews before being whisked to an afterparty by the other producers of the film. I didn't even have to change from my satin jumpsuit and heels, so I had to attend the party with what I had on.

While at the party I ran into a blast from my past. Devin Alexander.

Devin looked as if he hadn't aged a second. His custom-tailored suit fit him better than his skin. His dark hair was ringed at the temple with flecks of grey, and his tanned skin glowed like a light bulb was hidden beneath the surface. He had to be approaching at least 60 years old by now, but it was a rich 60.

Devin tugged at my arm. "Makeda, how are you doll?"

"Devin? So nice to see you, and unexpected too. This doesn't seem like your type of crowd," I remarked, referring to the hip-hop set.

He chortled. "You kidding me? I love hip-hop! But the real reason I came is you. Look at you, all grown-up and making something of yourself. Guess I was wrong in my assessment years ago, huh?"

I waved my hand dismissively, "Ancient history."

"Yeah, yeah, it is. I'm just glad you were able to recover. I was just sure messing with those thugs were going to be your undoing, but you proved me wrong."

I smile genuinely. "Well, thank you."

"From the moment I saw you in that club so many years ago I knew you were a star," he recalled. He was really pouring it on thick. I sensed he was setting me up for the kill. Laying on the charisma, then swooping in.

"So, what are you up to now?" Devin asked. "What are your plans? You have any more movies lined up?"

I deflected his question because I was ill-prepared for the next stage of my career. I didn't expect this much attention from the movie so I was befuddled. My manager and I had long parted ways. Since Haile swooped in, I'd pretty much followed him around, neglecting my career.

I asked Devin. "Why? You have something in mind?"

He smiled. "Do I have something in mind? Do I have something in mind? Don't I always have something in mind? I'm Devin Alexander! It hasn't been that long has it?" He joked. The he turned serious. "Are you being represented by anyone right now? What agency? Come on, tell me."

"I'm kind of between managers." I replied, not exactly lying.

He slapped his hands together. "Great!"

"Great?"

"Yeah! Haven't you heard? I represent certain actresses now too. I have a direct ear of some very important people in the movie industry now. You remember Lupe? The wetback that used to model for me when you were with us? Anyway, I was able to get her a role in some cheap Hispanic picture. The film ended up doing numbers! How 'bout that? Anyway, because of that, I extended the agency to include actresses on the roster."

I looked over Devin's head as if I was appearing to scan the crowd for someone more important, like my time was more valuable. All I could think about is how he bailed on me when I needed him most. What he was saying sounded good, but I also knew he wouldn't be talking to me if I hadn't taken my career into my own hands when he left me for dead.

"So?" I replied impatiently.

He clasped his hands together and slid them under my chin, just as he did the first night we met. "So, I'm feeling nostalgic," he said. "What say you come back onboard with the team? I have a line on a new movie that's about to begin production. I know you can get a major part in it. Put you right back on top. So?"

I pursed my lips to let him know I was at least contemplating his offer. Despite how he rejected me, I also knew how Devin did it. Big. And business was about relationships, not vendettas.

"Come on Makeda, look out for an old man, huh? All of you girls forget who helped you get started. Your friend Sophie gets married, knocked up, and pitches a home in the Carolinas. You go all Hollywood on me with your boyfriend— "

"Huh?" I cut him off. I thought I heard something that didn't make sense. "Wait, what did you say?"

"I said you've gone Hollywood on me."

"No, before that."

"Ohhhhhh. Your friend Sophie is pregnant now," he repeated. "You knew that didn't you?"

"Umm...no."

He slapped his forehead. "Ohhh that's right. She just told me yesterday. Said she was probably going to take off for a year to have the baby."

I hadn't spoken to Sophie in months. Our schedules weren't really gelling, but surely, she would have called me the minute she found out she was pregnant unless...

"She moved down south to South Carolina?" I asked Devin.

"North or South. Word is, she moved to be closer to her jailbird boyfriend. I tell ya, you girls sure know how to pick 'em." He shrugged his effeminate shoulders. "Who cares though? We're talking about me and you now. Are you coming home or what?"

Everything was coming at me so fast I just needed a second to process my thoughts.

"I'll call you about it next week," I promised. "Let's just enjoy tonight."

"Fair enough."

For the remainder of the night Devin and I partied for old time's sake, remembering K, and toasting to a bright future. I didn't think about the killer I shared my bed with, the war raging in the streets of my adopted hometown, or the drug-dealing mastermind I visited earlier. All I cared about was me.

And it felt good.

For a moment I wondered how life would be if I just focused on me. Fuck everybody else, just me. For all my life I'd deferred my dreams and happiness and bartered my future for the welfare of others. At 27 years old, maybe it was time for me to put me first.

I went to the bathroom to return some of the liquor I consumed. Only then did I notice my Blackberry kept vibrating. I wanted to ignore it and keep my party going but it was coming from a 404-area code. Atlanta. I thought maybe something might have happened to Haile, so I had to answer.

"Hello?"

"HOW COULD YOU LET HIM DO THAT?!"

I couldn't decipher the voice because of all the crying and screaming. "Hello?" I repeated.

"HE KILLED A BABY, MAKEDA. A FUCKIN' BABY!!!"

I finally caught the voice. "Tiffany?"

She sobbed uncontrollably on my line. Even amidst the throbbing base line pulsing through the walls, invading the bathroom, I could hear her tears as vividly as if she was in front of me.

"What are you talking about, Tiff?"

"You know." She cried. "You know exactly what I'm talking about."

"Tiffany, calm down. Tell me what you're talking about because I have no idea. And how are you calling me? Are you out?"

"Don't worry about it. Don't worry about me anymore. He's going down. All of them. You hear me? ALL OF THEM!"

My line went dead, leaving me more confused than when I answered. I tried to contact Haile all night, but he never picked up. I tried his second in command, the person who was designated troubleshooter should something occur, but I got no answer there either.

The whole scenario dampened my mood. I felt as if I was having multiple epiphanies but couldn't discern the multiple meanings. My life was going through an unwilling, unconscious metamorphosis that I was powerless to stop. I knew that a decision about who I wanted to be and what I really wanted to do with my life was rapidly approaching. At the moment, I was confused.

But I knew my answer was back in Atlanta.

CHAPTER 5

Makeda

The Nimrod Murders.

I must've been living inside a bubble for the past week because the headline was everywhere, and I failed to see it. I snatched two copies of the nation's most prominent newspapers from the airport bookstore and read the related articles a few times as I flew back to Atlanta. By the time I landed I was ready to kill Haile and take his head off. I'd sat by idly and even watched sometimes as he and his brother brought tragedy into the lives of others. But the way he did that 8-year-old was uncalled for. Now I knew why Tiffany was so upset.

I stepped out of baggage claim and saw Haile's white-on-white M6 BMW coupe sitting curbside. He spotted me and rushed to take my bags.

"Hey babe, how was the trip?"

I didn't even dignify him with a response. I walked past him and plopped down inside the baby-soft leather seat. Haile stuffed my bags in the trunk and came back to the car.

"Damn, what I do? A brother can't get a hug, kiss, or nothing?"

I cut my eyes at him.

"I said I'll make it up to you about not going with you to the premiere."

I said nothing. Haile pulled out into the late-night rush at Hartsfield-Jackson. As he maneuvered the coupe through pedestrian obstacles, he kept glancing at me. Finally, I couldn't take the silence anymore.

"Why did you have that little boy killed?" I yelled over the Dirty Red track shaking the ar.

Haile cut his eyes at me and twisted his mouth. But he said nothing.

"Haile?!"

He skidded to a stop right in the middle of traffic, killed the sounds with a button on the steering wheel, and just stared at me. People honked their horns all around us, but the Bimmer sat in place, V10 engine purring.

"What Makeda?"

I sighed deeply. "Why did you do that to those people?"

"What people?"

"The Nimrod Murders."

He chuckled. "Is that what they're calling it? Didn't think they were up on that," he mumbled. He tilted his head slightly to the side, chuckled again, then took off, smiling and shaking his head.

"He was a kid Haile!"

"Yo, don't give me that fuckin shit! I know what the fuck he was! I was there when he died. He didn't suffer. Aight? I choked him out in his sleep."

"But why!" I demanded, on the verge of tears. It was different when a kid was involved. I thought about my twins. They would've been just a few years younger than the boy. What if he would've did them like that?

"They were collateral damage," Haile attempted to justify. "In war, there's always collateral damage."

"Not kids though, baby. That's just wrong."

"Wrong?" He scoffed at me.

"Wrong is my man doing life in the Feds because a bitch he took care of can't hold her tongue. And don't get all new on me. Shit, you knew those fuckin' heads were in that bag when you went snooping that night. You didn't say shit then."

I felt like I was gonna be sick. That's where the blood came from. The sick bastard actually brought severed heads into our home as if he'd gone shopping for shoes. That could've been that 8-year-old boy's blood on my fingertips. I cringed at the thought.

Haile continued ranting. I could tell he was getting excited because the speed we were traveling had me pinned to the seat.

"What you need to be asking yourself is why they moved your girl out of jail into a safe house? You need to be wondering if she calling your name too?" He advised.

I thought about Tiffany's words ringing in my ear. 'All of them!' she'd said.

Haile dipped off I-285 onto I-85 and gunned the M6. After whizzing by light traffic, he took the exit for Jonesboro Road and piloted the Bimmer down the two-lane road breaking the speed limit by double. Just before we came to an intersection a big dump truck pulled in front of us, blocking our path. Haile pumped the brakes and the German super coupe crouched on all fours and came to a stop just inches from the driver's door of the truck.

"Motherfucka!" Haile swore, banging on the leather steering wheel. He blared the horn, then snatched the car in reverse, but another S.U.V was behind us, riding our bumper making it impossible for us to move.

Suddenly, two dark-colored sedans appeared on both sides of us like magic. I struggled to peer through Haile's dark window. As soon as the car came into focus, I glimpsed a long barrel thrust from the back window of the car on my side a split second before I ducked.

Everything happened so fast in the next second. The explosion from the barrel was so loud it snatched my hearing away and replaced it with a blaring ringing. Three golf-ball sized holes blew through the tinted window, raining shards of glass on my head. I screamed at the top of my lungs but couldn't even hear myself. The led storm drowned everything out. Blood splashed my cheek, throwing me into panic mode. I thought it was mine until I stole a glance at Haile. He was clutching his face, wincing. I heard automatic gunfire chattering, each round finding a home through the windshield.

"Stay down!" Haile barked at me, wasting precious breath. (Wasn't like I was going to sit up with shells whizzing through the car.) Haile whipped out a handgun from beneath the seat and returned fire right through the window on my side, then his. The shells ejected at a rapid pace and singed my arm before tumbling to the floor of the car. I clasped my hands over my ears, but the echoes still rocked my body.

Haile rammed the truck that was riding our back bumper twice, desperately trying to get some room to maneuver. He snatched the car from drive to reverse about twenty times in five seconds, but the bullets never stopped coming. The slide on Haile's gun locked back and I just knew we were dead.

Haile screamed at me pointing to the glove box, but I couldn't make out one word he said. Then suddenly, the lead shower relented just for a second and gifted me my hearing.

"THE GLOVE BOX!!!" Haile screamed, pointing. I popped it open and was met with an arsenal. Two mini-Uzis and more handguns just like the one he'd discarded lay neatly in the glovebox. I tossed him an Uzi and grabbed one of the handguns at the exact moment the cars flung another volley of rounds into the car.

Haile snatched the hammer back on top of the Uzi and opened fire through the broken window on my side while still ramming the Bimmer into the S.U.V behind us. The two vehicles locked into each other like magnets. Haile floored the pedal and 500 horses pushed into the S.U.V. Thick blue smoke clouded the interior, the pungent smell throwing me into a coughing fit. I covered my nose with the sleeve of my coat and watched as Haile sprayed the Uzi in a wide are through the windows. A mélange of smells competed for precedence in any mind. Burnt rubber. Gun powder. Fear. They all registered. None of them won out. Sensory overload.

We finally caught a break. Haile pushed the S.U.V back enough for us to find a gap to seep through. He wheeled through the gap in reverse, putting our killers in our front windshield. Only then did I sit up and survey the scene as the wind whizzed through the holes in the $100,000 car.

Of the two black Crown Vics that had us pinned in, only one remained mobile. It skidded around into a doughnut until the lone headlight faced us, paused, then barreled toward us. Haile slammed the Bimmer into drive and the coupe slung around in a one-eighty-degree arc. He punched the accelerator and we bolted into the cloudy Atlanta night.

Haile kept one eye glued to the rearview mirror and another on the highway, cursing and favoring his good arm. Blood trickled from his shoulder, painting the smooth white leather seats with its stickiness.

"Are you okay?" He asked me, scanning my body for signs of blood. "You hit?"

I shook my head. "Just glass, I think."

I looked over my shoulder. The Crown Vic appeared to be gaining on us. Haile saw my apprehension.

"Hold on," Haile said. He whipped the M6 into a narrow alley between two buildings. The car took the 90 degree turn as if it was on rails. A few seconds later the Crown Vic turned in behind us and clipped one of the buildings. Sparks flew from the bumper like fireworks. Haile smiled and gunned the engine. Beneath us the V10 growled and rocketed us forward until the headlight of the Crown Vic nearly became invisible. Haile slowed a little and smiled that sinister smirk of his. He mumbled something under his breath while watching the rearview.

We came up to an intersection of buildings and Haile snatched the park brake up. The M6 slid for what felt like a mile, then spun inside another alley perpendicular to us and stopped.

In one smooth motion Haile scooped up both Uzis and slipped through the driver's door.

"Don't move!" He barked at me.

As the Bimmer idled, my heart nearly beat out of my chest. Smoke still billowed inside the car from the cooked tires and the scent of gun powder mugged me. Meanwhile Haile hugged the edge of the building, clutching two Uzis as if he was the lead in a blockbuster movie. All I kept thinking was, *what the fuck am I doing here?* I heard the Crown Vic roaring up the alleyway. Just before it appeared in my sight, Haile stepped out into the alley and opened fire with both Uzis, one high, one low. Through the flashes of light, the muzzles created, I saw the drivers' heads open in a burst of blood and brains. The car crashed into the wall and stopped moving. Haile rushed the car and opened fire again until both Uzis were empty. Then he whipped his Desert Eagle out and approached the car slowly. The windows were all shattered enabling a clear view through the whole car. The back door opened and someone fell out barely holding on to a shotgun. Haile plugged him in the back twice before I could blink. But he was still alive.

Haile crouched down and snatched his head up by his braids. "Who sent you?"

The man choked on his blood as he attempted to answer. Nothing came out but blood.

"Who sent you?" Haile repeated. The man dropped his head in defeat. "Fuck it then!" Haile yelled. He popped two in his melon, then dashed back to the car, crouching low, scanning the alley for more targets.

He dipped back behind the driver's seat and tossed the spent Uzis on my lap.

"See what I mean." He remarked as we sped off. "In war there's always collateral damage. My fuckin' car, my arm...all of it is collateral damage because we at war. Even you. If I wasn't so good, you'd be dead. Collateral damage. Get my point now?"

CHAPTER 6

Makeda

After the attempt on our life Haile wouldn't let me leave his side. He took extra precautions by deploying tow of the top soldiers in the O.A.U. to pull around-the-clock guard duty on us. He even made me start wearing body armor and taught me how to use a gun. As fate would have it, while my man's crew was at war, my modeling and acting career was skyrocketing.

Calls came flooding in from as far as Japan from companies seeking my image for their products or wanting me to mode their clothes. Some of the top directors in California were calling me with offers for roles they wrote specifically for me. Devin blew me up three times a day for a week straight, but I didn't have the guts to return his calls and tell him I was being held hostage by my dangerous boyfriend.

I tried to explain to Haile that this was a once in a lifetime opportunity, that we could make a smooth transition out of the streets into a legitimate opportunity that could pay just as much. But he would have none of it. He was more stubborn than his brother was all those years ago. I felt like it was déjà vu all over again. No one received a second chance at this life, and here I was looking down the pipe at another opportunity. I'd once heard that life keeps sending the same lesson until it forced you to graduate to the next level or get expelled from life altogether. Thus far, I wasn't learning shit.

***

Around the first week of February, we found out Lil' Slim was back in Atlanta. His lawyers had filed a series of speedy-trial motions, so his trial was to begin the first week of March. Haile had made Slim's freedom his personal crusade. He had insinuated himself as the nucleolus of Slim's "legal" team outside the courtroom. He paid money to Slim's legal team and took meetings with the defense counsel to dig through his case file three times a week. The team seemed pretty confident that Slim would walk without K Mitchell around to corroborate his statements.

The only problem was Tiffany.

The government had moved Tiffany to a safehouse out of fear of her safety. After her family was murdered, she cut a record that would have the government's case against Lil Slim go platinum. The things she told made K Mitchell's statements seem like a pebble thrown into a tidal wave. Slim's defense team had mountains of paperwork from Tiffany's statements. Just as they would chop one set of papers down, another forest of testimony would be delivered to their office. Part of the reason why they were pushing for a speedy trial was so that the government wouldn't have time to bolster their case against Slim with more defectors.

The Feds had upped their surge on the streets, busting numerous SKG strongholds and trying to turn the members they captured. So far, their efforts were futile, but it was only a matter of time before they unearthed the weakest links. Most guys just weren't built to pull 25 to Life in the pen when just a few statements could spring them free.

While the Feds built their case for war, Haile wasn't sitting back and waiting on them to strike. He went on the offensive. First, he attempted to bribe the defense team with a shitload of money if they could find out and share Tiffany's location. They either couldn't find the location, or they weren't trying to become accomplices to Murder. Tiffany's testimony included numerous "allegations" of multiple murders "H" had committed at the behest of Slim's orders. Any attorney worth his bar card could put two and two together and figure out the "H" she referring to was probably Haile. I knew they sensed it. I could tell how they deferred to Haile that they were afraid of him. Because I was used to being around Haile, I was somewhat numb to his powerful, sinister presence, but I noticed how others reacted around him. His aura was dark and screamed he was not the one to cross. Just like his brother.

***

A few days before Slim's trial was set to begin, Haile was in the shower while I prepared us a meal. A stack of mail was on the table. I thought it was bills so I thumbed through the stack and saw a letter addressed to him from Menelik. The name was an alias, but I knew it was him. His address was Stevenson C.I. I recognized the place well. It was just up the street from where I did my time. Just holding the letter brought on waves of nostalgia. Curiosity overwhelmed me and I opened the letter.

According to the letter, Menelik had done well for himself. He'd started some type of arms company from back there and it was flourishing. He told Haile of a contract he'd just closed and mentioned how good his wife was treating him. She'd bought him an Aston Martin as a gift.

I felt sick when I read the word, *wife*. I read it again just so I wouldn't jump to conclusions. Sure enough, it was the same word the second time. *Wife*. Menelik was married, and apparently, his wife was his business partner. He only had seven months remaining before he maxed out his sentence. It seemed so long ago that he went away, so long since I removed him from my life. So long since I moved on with my life – in theory anyway. Truth was, I felt some type of way every time his name was mentioned. Reading his words made my heart skip a beat. His pretty cursive script reminded me of the letters he wrote to me over that year I was in his position.

I read on and the last line through me for a loop:

'Told you ole' girl wasn't shit. How about when she was in Jamaica, supposedly doing a shoot, she was getting fucked by some don over there. And get this: the bitch liked eating pussy too! Damn bro, best thing I ever did was get rid of her stank ass.'

At the end of the letter, he listed the website he could go to and see me getting down live and in color with this Jamaican don.

I shook my head, sat down at the computer, and waited for it to boot up so I could see for myself. While the computer did its thing, I thought about Menelik's letter. It seemed like he had matured into the man I wanted him to become. A piece of me was happy for him, but a part of me felt jealous that I wasn't by his side to assist in his transition, and I was willing to bet dollars to donuts who his wife was. I should've saw the signs a long time ago, but I was preoccupied with my own life. The unreturned phone calls, the lack of visits, always conveniently out of town when I was in her city, the way her mood changed when I would mention Menelik's name. It was all in front of me, but I chose to ignore the signs. Even Devin blared the news to me, yet I still chose to ignore it. *'Married and pregnant... moved to Carolina.'*

My friend had married my first love.

The computer finally powered up and I logged on to the site Menelik referenced in his letter. After a few seconds, an image of me popped up on the screen with a caption that read, "*Makeda's Ménage.*" The image showed only my face, twisted in a mask of pleasure and agony. I had to punch in a credit card number to see more.

A minute later, there I was live and in color on the screen getting pummeled from behind by a fat man while I ate Myomi's pussy.

My heart dropped as I watched the video and recalled the night well. I didn't exactly recall all that I'd done, but I remembered the party in Jamaica when they drugged me. Snatches of that night came back to me as I viewed the footage in awe and embarrassment. The portions I were unable to remember all these years were now filled in as I watched the tape. When Myomi came all in my mouth, I almost threw up on the desk. However, on tape, I seemed to be in heaven. The dazed look in my eye could easily be confused as pleasure when I knew it was the drugs that had me looking and behaving in that manner. Of course, no one would ever believe me. Public opinion was that all video models were hoes anyway. As the tape closed out, I wondered how long it would be before this was blown up and splashed all over the world. Or maybe it was already blown up and I was living in the dark? After all, Menelik had accessed the tape from jail. Maybe that was the reason the movie had me being promoted as the star and so many other directors were suddenly clamoring for me to appear in their films?

I heard Haile coming downstairs and I quickly exited the site.

"Babe you ready?" He asked me. We had a meeting with Slim's lawyers to go over his case one last time before the trial began.

"Yeah," I replied, shutting down the computer.

As we loaded into the bulletproofed S600 Benz with our escorts, I began to give my life some serious consideration. I pondered on the future I desired compared to the life I was living, and it all came back the same way. I wanted out of this life.

Now all I had to do was devise a plan.

CHAPTER 7

Menelik

I felt pain in my chest as if my heart was about to explode. My breath kept getting caught in my chest and wouldn't come up. The news that ignited the South and possibly the country had brought the biggest betrayal to my doorstep.

In the dayroom at Stevenson, I watched on the World News as the first day of trial began and the long line of entertainers and executives filed into the courtroom to show him support. The news kept calling him an entertainment mogul and alleged drug kingpin. Kept showing clips of him from various music industry functions. Showed clips of him showing off in front of his mansions and fleet of luxury and exotic vehicles, all courtesy of a street DVD he had produced.

Then came the other side.

They showed video footage of crime scenes allegedly orchestrated at the behest of Slim's. Beheadings, massacres, hangings...gruesome footage culled from police archives all over the country.

Then they showed footage of K Mitchell on set of his movie, directing. They showed video footage of K Mitchell and Slim at a party. Then they revealed footage of K Mitchell's murder scene, clearly tainting the court of public opinion with the insinuation. I knew they were going hard at him, trying to bury him, by the time this case was hogging up on World News. I was silently celebrating K Mitchell's death when the next footage knocked the wind out of me.

On the television screen they showed recorded footage of Makeda strutting inside the federal courthouse clutching Haile's hand. My eyes nearly bulged out my head. In the dayroom, all heads whipped their head in my direction, noting the uncanny resemblance between the face on the screen and myself. I tuned them out as the reporter identified Makeda as the red-hot model/actress with the checkered past. They identified Haile as her music executive boyfriend.

When I heard the reporter say the word, *boyfriend*, I almost fell out of my chair. I had to duck outside to catch my breath and run down my thoughts.

Now it all made sense. Haile wasn't answering my calls or my letters, ducking me as if I was some bitch he fucked and dismissed. I thought back to the last time he visited me before I left Perry. I'd asked him about Makeda and got stabbed in the side as if he was shanking me. *'Don't worry about her,'* he'd said. Now it all made sense.

I wondered how long they'd been fucking around. I wondered when she found out we were twins. Now I wondered if he killed K Mitchell to appease my hunger, free his partner, or to create space for him to swoop down and scoop up my bitch.

All kinds of thoughts whizzed through my head as I replayed every scenario in my past, fighting to decipher what was real and what was fake. I just couldn't believe my flesh and blood, the man I shared the same womb with, had backdoored me. No one could tell me he wasn't plotting the entire time, even back in New Jersey years ago. Who knew, maybe he had pretended to be me back then and slipped inside her goodness? Maybe he was fucking her back then and couldn't get enough? The pussy *was* good. But he's my brother. She was my girl, my first and only love.

And he just had to have her.

I tuned in to the World News every night after that first day, waiting to see their entrance. A part of me was hoping they wouldn't walk in together, like maybe it wasn't what I thought it was. But every day I watched the news, they strolled in holding hands with somber expressions. I couldn't deny how good Makeda looked each day. She sported classy skirt suits and high heels that befitted her model status. My treacherous other half looked just like a modern music executive with his custom-tailored low-cut double-breasted suits, neat thin braids, and huge diamonds in his earlobes. Together they looked like the perfect young successful couple, on display for the world.

To me, they were well-dressed traitors.

I watched the highlights of the trial for the first week on the nightly news. Later at night, I'd pull out my smartphone and log into the Atlanta-Journal Constitution's website and get in depth reviews and recaps.

Slim and his co-defendants had hired a legal defense dream team of the best lawyers on the East Coast. Slim himself had two of the best in the country, both out of North Carolina. Hamin Shabazz, an old school Muslim cat who had defended King Reece of the notorious Crescent Crew. The Crescent Crew were the SKG's predecessors. They ran the Southern drug trade until they escaped into the music industry and legitimized their riches. Hamin Shabazz had also defended Justus Moore, an alleged hitman who went on trial for murdering his woman's baby father and tucking his dick inside his mouth.

Slim's other attorney was a young black cat out of Charlotte, North Carolina named Theron Shields. Theron was the family attorney for the Padmore Family, a filthy rich crime family with political connections out of Charlotte. He was still riding high off a theatrical victory over a murder charge where two cops, an informant, and an illegal immigrant was murdered. Supposedly one of the Padmores was fucking an Assistant District Attorney on the case. Lately, it was the talk of the nation. Theron Shields was being touted as the next Johnny Cochran.

I read all this online. It was on Court T.V.'s website. In these types of cases, the attorneys were just as important as the defendants. Court TV also had footage of the courtroom. It appeared to be like a circus in there with Slim being the ringmaster catering to his audience. He seemed unaffected, as if his life wasn't on the line.

One night I caught a glimpse of Haile sitting proud in the front row. My blood boiled at the thought of his betrayal. I wasn't totally convinced his intent was malicious. I needed to see him and talk about things face to face. I had to make sense of the situation.

Unfortunately, that conversation would have to be put on the back burner for a long time.

Karma struck first.

CHAPTER 8

Makeda

For nearly a month I marched into the courtroom and watched the best the government had to offer try to bury a man who had come up from the grit of concrete and built an empire on fear, intimidation, and drugs. The man they characterized on the stand as a heartless, flashy, drug-dealing thug was a far cry from the man I grew to know. The Slim I knew abhorred violence and only used it when it was the absolute last resort. The Slim I knew was a charitable, fun-loving smart black man who chose to make something when the world gave him his ass to kiss. The violence and drugs just happened to be occupational hazards. But I knew the jury of his peers weren't going to do see it that way. The government was trying to make sure of it.

For the first month of a trial that was expected to last three months the federal prosecutors painted a broad stroke of Slim's tentacles. They had managed to infiltrate his bank records and on the twenty-fourth day of trial, an accounting expert took the stand and connected the dots. As he settled onto the stand, I couldn't help but notice how much he fit the perfect stereotype of a banker. He wore circular tortoiseshell glasses, his hair was shellacked to the side, and he even wore a yellow spotted bow tie beneath his neck.

The federal prosecutor dropped the lights down in the courtroom and pulled up a detailed PowerPoint presentation on the flat screens strategically placed all around the courtroom.

"Mr. Poindexter, how are you qualified to testify in this matter?" The prosecutor asked. The accountant rattled off a list of accomplishments. He had more degrees than I had sex partners. After running down his pedigree, the prosecutor continued.

"Mr. Poindexter, do you recognize the documents on that screen?"

"Um, um, yes," he pushed his glasses up on his nose. "They appear to be financial statements from Bank of America, and a few business accounts as well."

The prosecutor nodded. "Right, right." He flipped to the next page of documents. "And these?"

Poindexter identified the documents then elaborated on their use, explaining that criminal organizations use the forms to launder money into dummy accounts under commercial codes unknown to the masses. The prosecutor, whose name was Danny Crooks put up document after document for Poindexter to explain. After the third set of documents, I zoned out and focused on Crooks.

Crooks wasn't bad on the eyes at all. Tall, tanned, with brown hair that was cut into a military style. Long on the top, short on the sides with a sharp line up. His suit looked more expensive than the one Haile wore sitting beside me, which I knew was $2500—a discount since he purchased so many at once. Crooks finally finished showboating and turned the floor over to Slim's Dream Team.

Theron Shields took first strike with his fine ass. Theron stood only 5'8" and probably struggled to nip 160 pounds on the scale, but he carried himself like a giant. He was only in his early thirties, but he carried himself like a seasoned vet. He wore a grey three-piece suit with a deep red thick tie. The silky back portion of his vest was flecked with specks of red. Every time he sat down, he'd take off his topcoat to sport the vest and show off his toned physique. On a few occasions, I saw him glance over his shoulder and give me the eye, but I wasn't foolish enough to tempt the jealous nutcase beside me, so I didn't entertain him. Still, I was impressed by him and found myself wondering what it would be like to be his lady.

Attorney Shields walked right up to Poindexter on the stand and rubbed his waves a couple of times. "So, you're an expert, Mr. Poindexter?" He asked. The question came off like a smack in the face of his credentials.

"Umm...yes. The best, actually."

Theron nodded his head. "Okay, okay, the best?" He looked down at his black python skinned dress shoes as if the question lay between the tight grooves of the reptilian skin.

"So, tell me how many cases you have participated in like this, of this magnitude?"

"Well, um, none like this but —"

"How can you be so sure then?"

"—they're all the same."

"All the same?"

"Yes."

"So, do all black men look alike too?"

"Objection!"

"Sustained." The judge looked at attorney Shields with a warning in his eyes. "The jury will strike that last comment."

"Okay, I'm merely saying that just as all Black men don't look alike, all of these cases aren't the same," Attorney Shields clarified. "There are intricacies that defy presuppositions, realities that are more complicated than banking theories..."

Attorney Shield took the courtroom to school with big words that impressed everyone within earshot. He chiseled into the government's solid case, removing brick after brick with each question. By the time he was done, Poindexter appeared less of an academia and more like a common racist.

But Shabazz delivered the biggest blow.

Hamin Shabazz was the lead attorney for Slim. He was the one Haile sat with for hours and went over paperwork, corroborated some pieces of evidence so Shabazz could poke a hole in the facts, and totally dismissing other portions of the Discovery. If there was anyone in the courtroom who knew who "H" was, it was Shabazz.

Mr. Shabazz, as he preferred to be called, stood from the defense table, shot his cuffs protruding three inches from his suit jacket, and stroked his long red beard. The bright lights of the courtroom beamed off his brown bald head as he limped around to the witness stand.

"Mr. Poindexter," Shabazz whispered. "Are you familiar with the Santos Cartel?"

"I'm not sure I follow your question."

"Are you familiar with the Santos cartel out of Barranquilla, Colombia?"

Poindexter hesitated. Mr. Shabazz pointed at one of the flat-screen televisions. Instantly a picture of an obviously younger Poindexter flashed on the screen. He was standing next to a Latin man on a yacht, hamming up a good time.

"Are you familiar with Carlos Diamond Santos, head of the now defunct Santos Cartel?" Mr. Shabazz's voice boomed throughout the courtroom as if he was mic'd up. "And remember, you're under oath," he added.

Poindexter adjusted his glasses and looked deeper at the screen. "Oh. *That* Santos."

Mr. Shabazz nodded. "Hmm mmm...*that* Santos." Mr. Shabazz looked at the jury. "Well?'

"Well?"

"Do you know him or not, Mr. Poindexter?!"

"Umm...ummm... yes."

"Good, now we're getting somewhere." Shabazz turned and stared at Poindexter for a while before posing the next question. This must have been part of the plan they rehearsed because for the first time all week I saw Slim lean up in his chair with interest.

"Mr. Poindexter," Mr. Shabazz said, "Isn't it true you used to launder money for the Santos Cartel? Isn't that how you came to be such an *expert* on the subject, by doing it yourself?"

"Objection!"

Mr. Shabazz threw his hand up. A fresh document appeared on the flat screens.

"This is the deal you signed with the United States Government ten years ago! You agreed to debrief, and basically snitch, on the Santos Cartel in exchange for Immunity. Did you not?!"

There wasn't an eye in the courtroom that wasn't locked on that plea agreement blown up on 52-inch screens. Mr. Shabazz had posed a rhetorical question, for he knew the answer was live and in color. I remember thinking, *this is what a million-dollar defense looks like.*

The judge regained control of his courtroom and sustained the objection but the damage was already done. Mr. Shabazz had ripped into his façade and he wasn't letting up.

"I find it ironic that the man who invented these very elaborate financial machinations can now come to this Honorable Court and vilify them," Mr. Shabazz continued. "For all we know, you could be the mastermind behind this operation?"

Poindexter shook his head. "Absurd."

"We don't know."

"Th-th-that's crazy."

"You've done it before."

"B-B-but that was different!"

"What's so different? You were broke then?"

"I-it's just crazy."

"Objection! Badgering the witness."

"Why is it crazy? Does a leopard change its stripes?"

Finally, Poindexter snapped, "You can't possibly compare these... these... *guys* to the Santos Cartel! They're not nearly as sophisticated!"

Everyone in the courtroom fell silent. The lead prosecutor dropped his head in shame. Mr. Shabazz spun and shot a smirk at Slim, then faced the jury and bore into them, allowing the implications to seep in.

"Objection sustained," the judge ruled weakly.

Mr. Shabazz walked back to the defense table and sat down confidently. "No further questions."

After Poindexter faltered on the stand, the government introduced a few more pieces of evidence to try to salvage the money laundering side of their case, but even I could see they were grasping at straws. Their case hinged on Poindexter's testimony and the Dream Team busted him open like they were swinging at a piñata without the blindfolded.

Crooks settled down at the table behind mountains of paperwork. I'm sure he thought would nail Slim down with Poindexter, but as if he took on the attributes of his name, he squeezed right through the trap.

But they weren't done. Phase two was right around the corner and I'm sure they were gonna go even harder on the Murder and C.C.E. charges.

CHAPTER 9

Makeda

"It's just not a good idea for you to sit front row," Theron argued to Haile. "At least one of these witnesses can identify you and life can get real hard for you in a second," he reasoned.

Haile crossed his arms. His diamond cuff link found a sliver of light and beamed on the mahogany conference table. "Let me tell you something," Haile said, staring out the glass wall into the streets hundreds of feet below. "If they had something on me, I would've been picked up. Everything is just speculation, ya know."

We were in the Dream Team's office, preparing for the next phase of Slim's trial. One of the witnesses was a defector. He'd switched to the other side around the time Slim was picked up in New York. He was a low-level dealer in the organization, but he knew the hierarchy of the SKG, which is why he defected to the government when Haile returned to Atlanta and kept the SKG baking from left-over embers. He feared retaliation from the O.A.U because of his disloyalty. Word on the street said he was in the truck during the botched assassination attempt on Haile and me. However, this wasn't in his files.

"Do you want to get picked up and put on ice for speculation?" Theron posed.

"What are you saying?" Haile asked. He seemed to be giving Theron a lot of grief lately. I suspected he caught the not so-subtle glances Theron was pitching my way lately.

Theron shrugged. "Just saying we don't know how this thing is going to play out. I don't want to see you cased up alongside your boss."

"First of all, I'm my own boss! Got that?" Haile turned and gave Theron the full weight of his heavy stare. "And trust me, if the authorities had any idea who I was, you would be visiting me behind a steel door."

"Okay that's enough men," Mr. Shabazz intervened. He had been standing against the wall stroking his long beard, listening to the exchange. "If Mr. Jones here says he's fine, he's fine." He patted Haile on the back, as if they were old friends. "My only concern is how this guy's testimony can affect Mr. Slim. How about it, Mr. Jones? What do you think?"

Haile waved his hands dismissively. "Forget about him. I have a strong hunch this guy won't even show," Haile estimated with a smirk.

"What makes you so sure?" Theron queried, slightly agitated by Haile's smug demeanor.

Haile sucked up the attention, glad to be the man with a missing link amongst men who specialized in completing puzzles. "Let's just say the word on the street is he won't show," he answered cryptically.

"And you're going to hinge a man's freedom on a word on the street?" Theron scolded.

Haile dropped the smirk and the hint of play in his tone. He gave Theron his cold stare. "Okay, *I'm* saying he's not gonna show. Matter fact, I guarantee it."

Now we all caught the meaning.

Shabazz concluded the meeting with a frown. "Very well then, we'll focus on the detective and the agent."

***

"Agent Burch, could you please tell us exactly who you are and your relation to this case?" Crooks asked the man on the stand.

"As I said, my name is Paul Burch, I'm the Special Agent in Charge of the DEA's Southeastern Division, which covers Atlanta, Georgia, the headquarters of the Southern King's Gang. Later, as their operations grew, I was appointed Special Agent in charge of the Special Task force formed just to bring them down."

Crooks seemed really impressed with Agent Burch's pedigree. "How long would you say you've been investigating Mr. Singleton's organization?"

Agent Burch starred at the ceiling as if he was reading from an unseen script. "About five years," he answered.

"First came on our radar when he moved to Atlanta from Raleigh."

"So, is Mr. Singleton from North Carolina?'

Agent Burch shook his head.

"No. He's from Norman Park, Georgia, just outside Valdosta. He went to Shaw University on a basketball scholarship. He started his criminal enterprise in Raleigh and later moved to Atlanta when he grew in stature, probably after he got a new supplier, we believe."

"Objection. Speculation." Mr. Shabazz and Theron interjected simultaneously. Theron was watching Agent Burch as if he was prey while Mr. Shabazz scanned through some papers nonchalantly. Meanwhile Slim sat listening intently, stroking his goatee.

"Sustained. Please just testify to the facts," Judge Campbell advised.

"Agent Burch," Crooks pulled up another sheet on the screens throughout the courtroom. "Could you please tell us about this chart here?"

Crooks hit the remote and a hierarchy chart popped up on the screen. Pictures of members of the SKG were arranged in a box formation with Slim in the center. Some of the photos were mugshots, others were from surveillance clips and club flicks. A couple were even from magazines. A few of the members I saw a time or two. Most of them, I'd never seen a day in my life.

As Agent Burch began to break down the charts, I was amazed at just how much power and influence Slim carried in his lean frame. The SKG had soldiers in places as far as Cali, and as obscure as Colorado. They literally had a direct link to one of the most powerful drug cartels in the Western hemisphere, straight outta Mexico. A couple of major players inside the music industry were even plastered on the screen as suspected of doing business with Slim. Agent Burch made mention of the hip-hop cops and an audible gasp whooshed through the courtroom like the wave at a baseball game. I saw reporters from the major networks scurry out of the courtroom, probably rushing to be the first to break the story. For years it had been speculation, but Agent Burke had just confirmed the unit's existence. According to him, every city with a hip-hop presence had a unit and they all shared records.

Agent Burch broke down to the jury how Slim was getting his kilos for about $15,000 apiece and would sell them in bulks of ten for $19,000, virtually eliminating the competition. His coke also boasted the highest purity percentage, allowing his customers to easily make two-and-a-half kilos out of every one. He spoke of arrests following half-ton busts of coke on the highway, seizures of hundreds of thousands of dollars following the busts. As he itemized each incident, an accompanying image was flashed on the screens. It was one thing to hear about half tons of coke, it was another to see it! Blocks upon blocks of white, as if we were watching footage of ski slopes rather than drugs. The S.K.G. logo stamped so prominently on the blocks made it clear this was drugs though. The bundles of money were neatly wrapped in cellophane as if it was for sale in a grocery store. Millions of dollars of drugs seized!

Agent Burch told the court that the DEA busted one house and found $5 million behind the walls of the house. The money was apparently used to support the weak structure of the walls.

Unbelievable!

Then he broke each section of the SKG down by territory. Each man (and one woman) on the square controlled a section of the country. There was a Tye Black over the Missouri arm, Capone over Miami, L.B. over South Carolina, Slim's first cousin, T.J. in Raleigh. The names were too many to remember, but they were all rich well beyond the typical hood fare. And they all reported to Slim.

The whole time Agent Burch testified, Mr. Shabazz appeared unimpressed. He never bothered to take notes and the majority of the time he wasn't even facing the stand; he was closely observing the jury while braiding his long red beard.

Theron, on the other hand was crouched over the table ready to pounce. He was tense; I saw his jaw flexing from behind. He wanted Agent Burch bad!

But he would have to wait. Agent Burch testified the whole day—seven hours.

The next day Agent Burch introduced more evidence onto the record by way of his testimony, evidence that raised the temperature of the room considerably.

Crooks began with a simple question: "How did the S.K.G handle competition? How did they corner the market?"

Agent Burch sat up in the witness stand, cleared his throat, and addressed the court. "We noticed that a couple of years ago, their modus operandi changed. Before, they seemed to avoid violence. We heard Mr. Singleton said it was bad for business —"

"Objection. Hearsay!" The Dream Team barked in unison.

"Sustained. Only testify as to what you can prove, Mr. Burch."

Agent Burch nodded. "Well, once they set up operations in Atlanta they began resorting to violence—extreme levels." Agent Burch directed his attention to the TV screens once again. On cue, Crooks put more photos up. The first picture was so brutal I could barely look at it.

"Who is this?" Crooks asked.

"This is Rodney Watkins—or *was* Rodney Watkins." Agent Burch grimaced. "Mr. Watkins was the kingpin that ran the streets prior to the SKG infiltrating the drug trade there."

"And what happened to Mr. Watkins?"

"He was murdered obviously. As you can see by the picture, two to the back of the head, typical execution-style fare."

"And why is Mr. Watkins's death so pivotal to this case?"

Agent Burch sighed. "It's critical for a couple of reasons. First, Mr. Watkins's death served to cement a partnership between Mr. Singleton's organization and another rogue organization whom we'll get to in a minute. The rogue organization used to protect Mr. Watkins in exchange for a sort of street tax. However, when Mr. Singleton's gang came on the scene, they purchased their services, virtually employing an army to protect them. Mr. Watkins was the first casualty, a coup d'état of sorts."

"Now who is this organization that Mr. Singleton collaborated with?"

Agent Burch scratched his head. "They're called the O.A.U., which stands for *Organization of African Unity*."

My heart dropped to my feet. I nudged Haile. He leaned up closer to the defense table to listen harder. Theron glanced back at us with an uncomfortable look.

Agent Burch continued. "These guys are like vampires," he claimed, shaking his head. "They really are out for blood, but to this day, we can't get any direct read on them. All we know is they're from Africa. That's they're common bond. Judging from the tactics they use, we believe they're from West Africa, probably Nigeria."

Even I knew that was speculation, and subject to an objection but no one from the Dream Team entered an objection. They both listened intently while Haile finally leaned back and relaxed with a confident smirk on his face. The smirk quickly turned to a frown though as Crooks put up accompanying photos on the screens.

Gruesome would be an understatement. The remains plastered on the screens resembled animal carcasses rather than people. Bodies mutilated with bullet holes and stab wounds. Some of the bodies were missing limbs, others were missing their penises. Most of them were decapitated. The photos were vivid, homicide in 3D. As picture after picture flashed on the screen and the agent put names where facts used to be, it hit me hard. I had a flashback of all the death I'd seen, all the bloodshed at the hands of the only two men I ever loved. It was crazy but I could intuit which bodies Haile were responsible for. His jobs seemed more concise than the others. The bodies of his victims didn't have obscene holes puncturing the corpses. They were more precise, targeting specific areas of the body designed to incapacitate the victim. It was almost artful. But it was still murder.

"These guys are the real backbone of the SKG's success," Agent Burch proclaimed. "These villains struck terror in the hearts of would-be competitors. As you can see from the crime scene photos, limbs and heads are missing from the victims. Most of the time these body parts would be sent to the victims' families as warnings or as punishment for violating one of Mr. Singleton's edicts. He made sure that only his drugs were sold in Atlanta. If not, he would sick his band of killers on you."

More pictures of dead bodies flashed on the screen. I'd lost count around the 50th victim. As each still came up, the killings seemed to get more gruesome. I peeked at the jury box. A couple of the women out of the twelve couldn't stomach the carnage. As one of them puked all over the tiled floor, Crooks cracked a sinister smile at Slim, just before the judge ordered a brief recess.

During the recess, I looked at Haile closely to gauge his reaction to the damage he'd caused. He seemed numb, detached, as if he was watching a movie rather than his own work. Even though he hadn't committed all the murders, he was head of the O.A.U.; it was his orders that delivered death and heartache to the lives of so many. He may have looked like a handsome music executive to the rest of the world in his tailored suit and expensive reptilian footwear. He may have been called an aspiring mogul due to the way he was guiding Dirty Red's career to the top of the charts. But I knew better. He was already a mogul. A mogul of death. Worse than anything Menelik could ever be.

Court resumed and Agent Burch continued to paint the picture of death. More photos from crime scenes filled the courtroom as Agent Burch narrated.

"This picture here," he said. "Is significant for two reasons." He leaned over the stand and pointed at something in the photo. "This is a badge. Just on top of the badge is a diamond necklace with the initials S.K.G. on it. The necklace is estimated to be worth upwards of fifty-thousand dollars. It was left at the scene as a calling card of sorts. The victim was a police officer for the city of Miami. According to our sources, this officer was involved with a member of the Southern King's Gang's girlfriend, an exotic dancer. The woman wanted to call the relationship off with the gang member and marry the officer. Well, as you can see, the gangster had other plans. He murdered the officer while he was on duty, castrated him, then placed his expensive necklace on his neck to send a message."

"Why is that important?" Crooks asked.

"Well, for one, it's the first time we recorded a murder victim that wasn't drug related. I mean, as sick as it sounds, these guys seemed to abide by a code. They never targeted people that weren't in "the life" until then. It was also the first time they harmed a law enforcement official. You gotta remember, these guys were getting busted on the highway with millions in cash and drugs by regular traffic cops and never opened fire once. This killing was uncharacteristic of their modus operandi."

"Which meant?"

"It meant they were getting cocky," Agent Burch replied. He sighed deeply. "With a lot of these gangs, we notice a pattern. Once they own their territories, undisputedly, they tend to get a sense of invincibility. They become more violent and take bigger risks. We'd already seen what this gang was capable of, so we stepped up our efforts..."

As Agent Burch continued to ramble on the stand, I recalled all that I'd experienced while rolling with them. The private jets, exotic trips, Maybachs, poppin' bottles, all of it was the life I dreamed of living. A jet-setting lifestyle on my beauty, but for the last few years a whole bunch of ugly was financing my smiles. I never realized how much sadness and pain the lifestyle caused. I wasn't totally naïve; I'd seen a lot. I just didn't know the damage ran this deep. I just didn't feel the same about things anymore. The irony of the situation was that I was chest deep in the same lifestyle I'd chastised and abandoned Menelik about living.

On the stand, Agent Burch unearthed bones from a scene I knew all too well. Footage from K Mitchell's murder scene rolled on the screen. The mini mansion was torched beyond repair, but they were able to salvage K Mitchell's corpse. The government wasn't shy at all about showing the burned, mutilated corpse either. They wanted to drive home Slim's perceived ruthlessness. They wanted to parallel him to the devil.

"See this guy here?" Agent Burch said. "This was Mr. Singleton's business partner in his entertainment company. The man was a genius who wrote, directed, and produced his own films. Name was Kevin K. Mitchell."

"Why did Mr. Singleton allegedly have Mr. Mitchell murdered?"

Before Agent Burch could answer the question, a figure whizzed by us straight toward the defense table and tried to jump on Slim. It happened so fast, no one reacted quickly enough. The woman dived right on Slim screaming, "MURDERER!!! You took my son's father!"

Haile dashed to the rescue and yoked the women up from behind before the armed bailiffs moved. It was almost as if they wanted the woman to attack Slim. Haile tossed the woman in the bailiff's arms like she was a rag doll. Meanwhile, Slim stood and fixed his clothes. Drops of blood trickled from the scratches on his face the woman managed to inflict. As she was carried away in handcuffs, she threw optic daggers my way.

"You should be ashamed of yourself! You was in on it. I know it!" She ranted. She hawk spit at me, just barely missing my $2,000 Louboutin's. Haile jumped at her, but a bailiff intervened to settle things down. The judge banged his gavel (a little too late if you ask me) and barked on everybody with his stocky glare.

"If anybody else moves past that galley partition that does not have something to do with this case, they will be shot," he promised. I didn't know if he was serious or not, but no one dared test his limits.

Court resumed and Agent Burch answered the question that was on everyone's mind. I still wasn't completely convinced K had turned informant. I mean, yeah, he was more bitch than any model I'd ever seen but Slim had done too much for him for him to rat him out. Or so I thought.

"We managed to successfully turn Mr. Mitchell against Mr. Singleton's organization," Agent Burch confirmed as soon as court resumed. Oooh's and ahhh's sprouted up around the courtroom.

"No one we captured would turn against him, but we found a willing mole in Mr. Mitchell. He was undercover for about a year, around the time he first set up his company in Atlanta. We somewhat aided him by granting him requisition forms for a Ferrari and an expensive condominium lease. You see, he had to look the part to stay on Mr. Singleton's radar. It paid off because he eventually managed to infiltrate the gang and was able to provide us names, dates, locations, routes.... pieces we never could've figured out without his assistance."

Haile tapped me and whispered, "Told you the nigga was a rat."

I shook my head. I couldn't believe it. A real rat! All this time.

So, what happened to Mr. Mitchell?" Crooks asked.

"Apparently, he was discovered, and is the pattern with this gang, murdered before he could corroborate his statements in court. However, we did take a deposition which sadly, can't be used."

"Objection, your honor!" Theron shot to his feet. "The witness is obviously attempting to taint the jury. He knows we had hearing covering that deposition. Now he's trying to use its in admissibility to taint the jury."

Mr. Shabazz stood and peered around the courtroom with indignation. "Your Honor, at this time we're going to have to request that you declare a mistrial."

Crooks whirled around to face the Dream Team and squealed, "A mistrial? Your Honor, the witness said nothing that a curative instruction couldn't correct."

"I disagree."

"Me too," Theron concurred. "The jury is tainted."

"They're not."

"They are too."

The sides bickered for a moment like kids. Meanwhile K's image remained transfixed on the huge screens. All types of memories fought with my confusion and stupor. I kept analyzing what was real and what was fake. *All this time K was an informant?* I'd jumped from the strongest type of man to the lowest form of a man. Menelik was a man with principles and integrity, with a method to his madness. K was the complete opposite, a peon that bit the hand that fed him. I just couldn't shake the Trenton side of me that taught no snitching. Despite the love I once held for K, I was now disgusted with him.

We stepped outside the courthouse amidst total chaos. The sun was just beginning to set casting a picturesque view in the sky. Reporters were taking heed to us as their cameras flashed non-stop. Microphones were thrust into one Maybach, while Haile and I climbed into ours with the bulletproof exterior. From court, we would always head to an expensive restaurant to discuss the day's events, brief for the following day, or just chill and relax a bit.

However, this day was different.

As we descended the steps, the reporters would not allow us to leave. They cut our path off and kept asking Dr. Shabazz about the defected witness. Eventually our security emerged to clear a path. As we hurried to the visitor parking we noticed a bunch of commotion centered around a 7-series Bimmer. Police had erected a barricade around the car with their police cruisers. The lights from the cars lit up the parking lot in bright blue hues, but their sirens were silent. I tried to peer hard and see who had gotten trapped off. Friend or foe? Haile tried to see also. I thought it might have been someone from the gang.

We settled into the back of the Maybach and Haile instructed the driver to take us past the commotion so we could inspect it further. As the Maybach crept by the parking lot, I got a closer look. As I should've predicted, there was more carnage. Placed neatly atop the roof of the Bimmer was a severed head. The ears were missing, the eyes had been poked out, and the mouth appeared to be stapled shut. Blood was caked all over the face which told me whomever did this to him had inflicted the messages while he was still alive.

Chills zipped through my body.

"Welp, guess that's that with that," Haile quipped craning his neck to get a close look. He pointed at the back of the Bimmer. "Look at that."

The license tag read: D. Crooks.

CHAPTER 10

Menelik

The detective came to see me early that morning. *They finally caught up with me,* I thought. I knew it had to be serious because Lieutenant Brady had come to escort me up front. He wouldn't leave me alone for a second either. He watched as I washed my face, brushed my teeth, and dressed in a clean uniform. He stayed near my side as we walked on the yard. In all honesty, Stevenson only had one chain-link fence with a thin strip of barbed wire across the tip. If I wanted to get rabbit, I could've easily disposed of Lieutenant Brady and became a ghost.

But I was too close to freedom for a life on the lam.

We entered the control room area and I tensed up. The detective was standing there awaiting my arrival. I could tell that he had heard of my exploits because his body language changed as soon as I bent the corner. His white face had a deep tan and his tan suit was a little too tight to be stylish, but his shoes were expensive, although basic. (Sophie had me zoning in on everyone's shoes now. Said it told a lot about a person.) Lieutenant Brady and the detective led me into the warden's conference room upstairs. I knew it was serious then.

Lieutenant Brady stood guard at the door while I took a seat at the head of the table. While I sat, the detective stared at me in silence with his grey eyes. Inside, my heart galloped in my chest, my mouth dried up, and I fought to appear calm on the outside. I kept thinking, *is this the one they sent to put me in a box forever.*

The detective took the seat at the opposite end of the table, spun it around, and sat down with the back of the chair on his scrawny chest.

"So, Mr. Menelik, right? Thomas Menelik?"

Over the years I'd grown accustomed to my alias. When I'd had the driver's license forged, J.L. Gore suggested I keep my first name so that when I was called by my alias, I wouldn't look surprised or unnatural. Since I'd always been known in the streets by one name, I just flipped it.

"That's me," I replied.

"My name is Special Agent Randy Bills. I'm with the Federal Bureau of Investigation. Today I want to speak with you about a murder."

When he said F.B.I. I just know I was through! It took everything in me not to show any emotion. Keep my face poker. My eyes darted around the room, visualizing possible escape routes while he spoke.

"I'm going to call out a few names," he said. "If you recognize any of them, nod yes. Got it?"

I nodded.

"Jamie Livingston? And you better nod your damn head on that one."

I nodded. Jamie Livingston was J.Y., the snitch I was serving time for shooting.

He went down the line rattling off a list of names. Then he struck gold. "You ever heard of J.L. Gore? Huh? You ever hear of any of these people?"

I shook my head again and again and again.

"Oh, you don't know any of them?" Agent Bills was up and down the table in flash. He tossed a picture of all the people he inquired about onto the table. J.L., and J.Y. J.Y.'s picture was taken while he was in the hospital after I shot him.

I shook my head and pointed to J.Y.'s picture. "The only one I know is him."

"Livingston?"

I nodded, "Yep."

"Did you kill Livingston?"

"I tried to."

"You don't know anything about his death?"

I shrugged my shoulders. "I wish I did, but there's nothing I can tell you."

He pointed at J.L.'s picture. "And you don't know him?"

"Nope."

"Sure?"

"Yup."

"Positive?"

"Yep."

"So, why do we have a statement from Gore saying he sent you down here from Jersey to take Livingston out?"

"Jersey?" He was getting too close for comfort. I had to push him off. "That's crazy? I've never been to Jersey," I lied.

"So, it's just a coincidence that Livingston was decapitated in the same manner that you disposed of J.L. Gore's competition back in Jersey."

"I never been to Jersey."

"BULLSHIT! We got people that can place you in Jersey!" He crouched near my ear and whispered. "You ever hear of the Caravan?"

My heart paused in my chest but outwardly I remained poker faced. The agent knew he had struck a home run though. He stood, cackled, and began to taunt me.

"Yeah, ole bad ass Menelik! We finally caught up with your ass. You can run but you can't hide. It took us a while but we finally got your ass. The Caravan, Born, his brothers... you gonna pay for all that shit. And guess what else? We got a live tape of you killing my comrade. For that, we gonna push a needle in your arm, courtesy of the U.S. government."

I refused to let him see me bend. He had the pieces, but his puzzle wasn't together. He was missing something, otherwise he would've taken me into custody already. Feds overruled the state, and federal murder trumped my conviction. I was due to max-out my sentence in under six months. If he was that confident, he had something on me, he would've definitely snatched me up.

"I've never been to Jersey," I repeated. "And I never killed anyone." I had trouble keeping a straight face when I told the last lie. I had no clue how many people I had murdered for profit.

"And if you're so sure of something different, why don't you take me into custody?" I challenged and held my hands out for him to cuff me.

"Oh, I will," he promised. "Just a matter of time. I know you're guilty, and I will prove it. I just wanted to look you in your eyes and tell you what I was going to do first. I want you to shake in your boots like you made so many others shake in theirs. But you better believe your ass will never breathe the air of a free man again."

"Good luck with that."

"Good luck to you. You're gonna need it, you fucking prick."

The agent dismissed himself. After he left, Lieutenant Brady and I remained in the warden's conference room and chatted.

"Yo gonna be alright, Menelik?" He asked. "You need any help. Need to call your wife?"

Lieutenant Brady had been on my payroll for a while. He had brought in my cell phone, DVD player, and regularly bought me food in from the outside. On occasion, when he was over the yard on weekend shifts, he would let me use his office to make love to my wife. For his services, I had damn near paid for his new Toyota Tundra over time. A hundred dollars here, a couple hundred there. It all added up. My new business venture was making me a wealthy man, and I wasn't shy about sharing my wealth to make my incarceration bearable.

"Nah LT, I'm straight. Thanks though."

"No problem." Lt. Brady crossed his arms and kicked a foot up on the wall. "You seem kind of calm for an innocent man, Menelik. You sure you ain't do none of that stuff?"

I shot him a knowing smirk. "I know they can't prove I did any of it. That's all that matters."

"Well, you better be careful, then. If them crackers came all the way here to see you, they got something. And if they can't prove it, they will pin it on you," he warned.

I filed away his warning and returned to my cubicle.

Later that night, I fished out my phone and dialed a number I hadn't called in a long time. He answered on the third ring.

"Hey Uncle," I greeted. "I've made some bad moves and I need your help."

CHAPTER 11

Makeda

After the witness was murdered in brutal fashion, security was heightened at the trial. Out of fear of losing any more witness, the trial was accelerated. The government rushed a few more witnesses through the stand to attempt to bolster their case, but Theron Shields ripped through them like a rabid Wolverine. They were so inept Dr. Shabazz didn't even cross examine then. He left that all up to Theron's sexy ass! Everything about him exuded class and power, from his snug fitting tailored suits to his southern drawl. He lit up the courtroom as he berated the witnesses. Every so often, I caught him checking me out on the sly.

One day after leaving court, Haile reminded behind with Dr. Shabazz while Theron and I went ahead to the restaurant to secure the reservations. We were in the Rolls Royce Phantom this day, so there was no partition between us as the driver piloted us to the restaurant. We rode in silence for nearly fifteen minutes, me on my side of the car and Theron on his. Out the blue Theron started talking.

"This the kind of guy you like?"

I was shocked. "Excuse me?" I whispered, continuing to gaze at Atlanta whizzing by my window.

"This H character," he said. "This your type?"

I sighed, "Why? What's wrong with him?"

Theron shrugged his shoulders. "Nothing, if that's what you like," he replied cryptically.

I turned toward him and pulled my shirt down over my knees. I wondered if he knew I starting to get wet as soon as he sat in the car.

"What are you trying to say, Mr. Shields? Got on with it."

Theron closed the folder on his lap and turned toward me. "It seems to me that a famous model and actress such as yourself could have any man she desires, but you're spending your time with that gangster."

"Gangster?" I scoffed. "Haile is not a gangster. He is in the music business."

"Yeah I know – he creates symphonies of death," he sniped.

"You must have him mistaken," I denied.

"Sure, okay, whatever you have to tell yourself, but we both know his days are limited," Theron estimated. "Then what? Can you stand another stretch in prison? What about your career? Are you prepared to do life?"

I stopped him. "Wait a minute! What do you mean by all this? I mean, even if Haile was a gangster as you claim, that's his life. What does that have to do with me?"

Theron eyed me with pity. "I know you're not that naïve, Ms. Barnes. I can't tell you how many cases I've seen where wives go to jail along with their husbands for Collusion, Complicity, and Conspiracy, just for spending illegal money. Sometimes, the man would scapegoat his woman and he wouldn't do a day in prison," he explained.

"Haile's not like that!" I protested. "He would die for me."

"Or maybe kill for you too huh?" His implication was clear. He was referring to K Mitchell.

"Wait, whose side are you on anyway? Why are you telling me all this?"

His eyes locked on mine and held me in his gaze for a few seconds. I'd never noticed how thick his eyebrows were or how dark and enchanting his eyes were either. I felt my juices began to trickle inside my inner thigh.

"I am on Slim's side in the court room," he clarified. "Outside the courtroom, I have my own agenda, and in that capacity, I absolutely hate to see a woman throw her life away for nothing. Especially a woman as beautiful and talented as you."

When he touched me, my leg sizzled. Good thing we were pulling up to the restaurant. Haile was already there waiting on us. I saw his black-on-black Ferrari Scaglietti shining in front of the door. As soon as the Phantom stopped, he jerked open my door and pulled me out the Rolls Royce. He guided me inside to the table where Dr. Shabazz was already seated.

I couldn't recall what we ate that night because while they talked legal mumbo-jumbo, my mind was digesting Theron's comments. His words were eerily reminiscent of K Mitchell's warning so many years ago about Menelik. Ironically, it was K Mitchell's work that had me on the cusp of stardom. Was he speaking from the grave? Devin had been calling non-stop with lucrative opportunities. A few notable directors were trying to contact me. Tyler Perry's studio had even reached out to me in the past week.

But I was stuck to Haile's side like Velcro.

During dinner, Theron kept tossing not so-subtle glances my way. I was sure Haile caught a few of them. Theron must didn't know how dangerous Haile really was! He had a jealous streak longer than I-95. Midway through the meal, Haile abruptly pulled me up from the table.

"Let me speak with you a moment," he grunted.

He led me outside to his Ferrari, posted up boldly beneath the awning so he could stunt on everyone. As soon as we settled into the hard Italian leather seats, he started grilling me.

"That smart country muthafucka didn't try to get slick, did he?"

"Who?" I frowned, feigning ignorance.

"You know who! That fuckin' lawyer."

"Oh. No, baby he didn't," I lied smoothly.

"You sure?"

"Of course not. He knows where my heart lies." I assured him. Haile was like a bloodhound. Any scent of deception and he would lock onto it and sniff out the violations. Then he would violate them.

"Oh ok." Haile sighed and leaned his tall frame back into the seat. He pinched his nostrils and closed his eyes.

I reached over and rubbed his head. "You okay?"

He nodded. "Just stressed."

"Aww I know just what will make you feel better," I cooed. I reached down and unbuckled his grey pin-striped trousers. I wanted to put his mind somewhere else. Get him away from his suspicion. Assure him of my place in his life and my loyalty.

I struggled to pull Haile's emerging erection through his tight boxer-briefs. I finally managed to fling it through the hole of his boxers and hold it in my hands. Even through the dim lighting illuminating the cabin, it still appeared to dominate the small confines of the car. Even now after years of riding it, sucking it, and feeling it, I was still in awe of Haile's dick. It was a masterpiece.

"That's feels good, baby," he grunted as I stroked him.

"Hmm? Really?" I felt him nod his head. "Well, you're gonna love this."

I placed him inside my mouth and sucked him real slow. In and out. He grunted his pleasure each time I took him deep inside my jaws as, outside the car, people walked by slowly, admiring the quarter-million-dollar machine. Just the possibility of a nosy spectator pressing his face against the glass to look inside enlivened me. I tooted my butt up in the air and really got down on it. Haile loved it too. He hiked my skirt up and rubbed my ass while I sucked his stress away. One of his fat fingers found the edge of my opening and toyed with my warm moisture while I tried to take all of him inside my mouth.

I felt Haile about to erupt. I wasn't too thrilled about adding extra flavor to my meal, but he was my man, so I had to oblige him. Anything for my man.

I caved my jaws in around the head of his dick and pulled back slowly. Haile began thrusting his hips up toward my mouth.

"Shit baby! Shit baby! I'm 'bout to cum," he moaned. "Awww. Fuck!"

He poured what felt like a gallon of babies in my mouth. I tried to swallow them all, but some accidentally leaked out right onto his thousand-dollar pants.

"Oh shit, Haile!" I shrieked cupping my mouth to keep any more spillage inside. "It's on your pants."

He gently nudged me aside and sat up to inspect the damage. "Aww it's no biggie," he claimed, and opened the door. "Let's go back and get some dessert.

As we walked back to the table, I checked to see if a spot was on his pants. Sure enough, a thick cum spot was right near the top of his pants, just beneath his topcoat. Haile swaggered to the table as if it wasn't even there.

"We weren't gone too long, were we?" He asked. I saw Theron's eyes dart straight to that wet spot, then he frowned.

"Nah, not at all," Dr. Shabazz said. He clasped his hands together. "However, I do have to get going. I have a long night with some new paperwork I just received today. Mr. Slim's girlfriend's case file was just delivered to my suite. And it's a monster."

CHAPTER 12

Makeda

The following morning, Dr. Shabazz summoned Haile and I to his hotel suite downtown. It was a Saturday and Haile and I were still in the studio sleeping quarters. We had sat in all night on Dirty Red's recording session for his new album. The album was near competition, so Haile had to make sure the material was sellable. With all that was going on, the studio was the one place that gave Haile solace it seemed.

We slipped on some comfortable clothes and I piloted Haile's 600 SL Benz to the hotel while we listened to a rough cut of Dirty Red's progress. Haile counted stacks upon stacks of hundred-dollar bills, before placing the rubber banded stacks into a LV messenger bag. The music was bumping so hard, the big-black pistol sitting on his thigh vibrated as if a heartbeat was thumping inside the hard plastic. On the floor, resting between his right Air Jordan sneaker and the door was a Heckler and Koch machine gun with a long banana clip poking out awkwardly. When I was younger, I wouldn't have thought twice about all the danger encircling me. Hell, it probably would've turned me on! Now, approaching 30... as a successful model with a budding acting career... it just didn't feel as if I was on par with my life's purpose. I knew this is not where I should've been. I loved Haile a lot and I was grateful for all that he'd done for me, but what are the limits of love? What are the limits of loyalty? At what part do you abandon the Titanic, a big luxury cruise headed toward certain disaster?

My mind whirred, processing and sharing my emotions, weighing the pros and cons of my situation, contemplating if, when, and how I could exit stage left before I became the next victim on a long, bloody, nameless, faceless parade. No matter how I broke it down, it never ended pretty.

It got even uglier when we entered Dr. Shabazz's suite.

Dr. Shabazz greeted us at the door of his opulent suite already dressed in expensive slacks and a white tailored striped shirt with huge diamond cuffs links. Even his socks that he glided across the floor in looked expensive. The suite itself was elegant, but boxes of papers, discs, and a few computers littered the space. He cleared a space on the sofa and directed us to sit down.

"Good morning Haile and Beautiful," he said with a slight bow. "Coffee? Breakfast? Anything?"

Haile grunted and shook his head. "We good," he croaked, answering for me.

"What's up? Why'd you call us here?"

Dr. Shabazz chuckled. "Don't waste much time, huh?"

"Time is money," Haile quipped.

"That it is, son. That it is." Dr. Shabazz sighed and turned one of the computers to face us. On the 21-inch screen was an image of Tiffany's face, frozen in time. "Recognize her?"

"That's my best friend!" I piped up quickly. Just seeing her face smacked me with memories of the time we spent together. Good times. Before all the madness of the paths we chose ripped us apart and placed us on opposing sides.

Haile looked at me as if he wanted to break my neck for acknowledging Tiffany and I shared a past.

"Yeah, I know the bird," he replied, contempt apparent in his voice.

Dr. Shabazz nodded. "She knows the both of you two pretty good. And before I say what must be said, I think it's imperative you watch this video while I finish eating breakfast," he suggested. "It's only about thirty minutes or so, but the information could last a lifetime. A lifetime."

Haile and I settled in front of the computer. Dr. Shabazz started the video then left us alone while he finished his egg whites, toast, and baked salmon, just a table over from us.

On the screen, Tiffany's face seemed more fuller, and her hair shined in the light. Her hazel eyes blazed above heavy bags. Her glossy lips and pouty mouth opened and spit out a life sentence.

She first told about how she and Slim first met. Then she told about the lavish trips out of the country and the lavish lifestyle she shared with Slim. Just hearing her words recalled the wonderful times balling out with the crew. Then she painted a picture of drugs, death, retaliation, and heinous acts of murder. She put me on the bus with her on some of the trips. Then she threw me under the bus with the crimes she knew I witnessed. She told them my boyfriend was the most dangerous man she'd ever met in her life. Near tears, she briefly recounted murder after murder that she personally witnessed Haile commit — and she told them I was with him for more than a few killings. The person administering the deposition stopped her squealing and asked her a question.

"*This girlfriend,*" he said, out of view from the camera. "*Is this the supermodel, Makeda Barnes?*"

Tiffany nodded her head vigorously. "Yes, yes," she replied in tears. "It is her."

I could see the pain of her admission etch onto her face, as if she felt terrible for putting me out there. But she still did it. I recalled her threat just as a cold shudder trickled through my body. Beside me, I felt Haile flinch up as if he wanted to jump through the screen and choke her to death. Meanwhile, she continued spreading her treason.

"What can you tell us about Kevin "K" Mitchell?" Someone asked. Tiffany straightened up and spilled her guts.

According to her, K Mitchell had confided in her that he was afraid of Haile because he knew that Haile had a huge crush on me. She claimed that during the time K and I were together, she caught Haile and I having sex. I had no clue why who I was fucking had anything to do with Slim's case, but then the answer slowly rose to the surface.

Motive. They were trying to establish a motive.

Tiffany went on for a few more minutes with her taped snitching before the investigator asked two more questions that shook my shoes.

"Would you be able to identify this H guy?" They asked.

"In my sleep."

"Would you be willing to testify in court?"

Tiffany paused a moment and then answered the question. "If I live that long."

Then the tape went blank.

Haile and I sat stunned to silence. Once again, I saw my modeling career imploding. Ironically by the person who helped rebuild it. I recalled my days at Camille-Graham prison and shuddered at the recollection of how burned Jack Mac smelled. I felt that empty feeling, pangs in my gut, the jitters. Felt the coarse material of institutional panties cuffing my fat pussy.

I refused to go back to prison.

"That deposition was taken a few months ago," Dr. Shabazz said from the table. He stuffed a forkful of eggs into his mouth, then stood and wiped his hands before walking over to us.

"I was able to get an inadmissible ruling on it because she refused to come to court to corroborate it," he explained. "Well, now that she has agreed to testify, we don't need the video. She's ready to say everything she said on that tape on the stand. And then some," he added.

Haile clasped his hands and placed them under his mouth as he stared off into space.

"I don't get it," he said, tilting his head. "If they have all this, why didn't they pick me up yet? I mean, I'm there every day."

Dr. Shabazz didn't seem affected by Haile's admission that he was the infamous "H" referred to so ominously in numerous court documents. I'm sure he suspected it, but suspicion and confirmation are two different arenas.

"My guess." Dr. Shabazz said as he paced the floor. "Is that they're afraid of the retaliation from your comrades. Sounds weird, but as long as you've been attending this trial, there has been less violence in the streets. If they haul you in, who's going to be over your gang? Who is going to keep them civil? As crazy as it sounds, they need you free...for now."

Haile bounced to his feet. "Oh. And then what?" he posed, pacing in the opposite direction of Dr. Shabazz. The two of them looked like two boxers sizing each other up.

"Or..." Dr. Shabazz froze and held up his finger. "They're watching you and waiting on you to slip up so they can catch you red-handed and POW—" He punched his left fist into his right palm, then whispered. "They got you."

This guy is good, I thought. Haile paced the floor in deep contemplation. I could see the chess match going on inside head. I could see him weighing options, dismissing frail plans, and dissecting the stronger ones. Mentally sacrificing pawns while repositioning his rocks. Was he thinking about protecting the Queen though?

Dr. Shabazz intersected Haile's path and tapped him on the chest. "Take a seat young brother, let me share something with you that may make you see me different and help ease your mind a bit."

Dr. Shabazz pulled up a chair and grabbed his coffee mug. He bent over to show us a tiny scar in the back of his bald head. "You see this right here?" He pointed to the scar. "I got this protecting a client with a job just like yours, H. A woman that was attempting to assassinate him tried to execute me also. But I didn't bend or break. And I never told anyone, especially the authorities."

Haile seemed unimpressed. "So, what's your point, doctor?" He asked.

"My point is that I never betray the confidences of my clients."

"Ok?"

"I'm telling you that whatever is said here stays here. I'm also telling you that I strongly advise you not to go into that courtroom today while Ms. Gauge is testifying."

Haile seemed to contemplate for a moment. He looked off into the sun steady rising through the glass wall of the suite.

"If you're saying they don't want to bring me in yet, then what's the harm in me showing up?" He posed.

Dr. Shabazz appeared to measure his words carefully before he spoke. He took a sip from his mug emblazoned with a crescent and a star on the side, then replied, "There's no way to determine Ms. Gauge's reaction once she sees you. She is death-scared of you, and the federal prosecutor knows it. He may move on you just to protect his case because – trust me – she is all he has left."

I could see where he was coming from. Tiffany was the star witness now, the one who could connect all the dots. Considering the recent murder and public display, they may attempt to haul him in for safe keeping.

I rubbed Haile's broad back whispers in his ear. "Maybe he's right, babe. Maybe you can just lay low for the day."

He recoiled his neck. "Lay low? What the fuck does that mean? Lay low...I'm about action! My man Slim needs me there," he insisted.

"No Slim needs you here, out here," I corrected him. "Feel me?"

While I attempted to calm the beast, Dr. Shabazz pretended to go over paperwork. Haile and I went back and forth, but eventually reason won out. He decided to lay low while I went to show Slim support for the both of us.

An hour after I left Haile, I was in the front row of the galley pumping my fist at Slim to show him my support. Deep down inside, I really did want Slim to walk free. He was a good guy and loved to live life to the fullest! The Slim I knew was nothing like the monster the courts portrayed him to be. Even in the shackles of the "shit-stem" Slim still shined bright like a diamond in his grey suit and cognac-colored shoes. His slim frame had filled out a bit and his face looked so full. He had cut his braids, revealing a head full of soft tight curls. He smiled warmly at me and nodded his head knowingly, as if he already knew why Haile was missing. I suspect Dr. Shabazz had already informed him.

The judge called court into session and an eerie silence cast over the room. One witness was set to testify before Tiffany took the stand. The courtroom was stuffed with more people than usual, the wolf pack known as the media eagerly anticipating the worst. Just as I crossed my alligator pump over my knee, I felt someone tap me on the shoulder. It was a U.S. Marshall.

"Ms. Barnes?"

I ate the lump in my throat. "Yes?"

"You need to come with me please."

All eyes were on me as I followed the tall white deputy out of the main courtroom into a large conference room. He used a wand to search me first, then patted me down with his hands. I'd long learned to hold my tongue unless my attorney was present, so I stood silent as an assassin on stakeout.

"Please, sit" the Marshall instructed. I sat at the long wooden conference table, nerves in disarray. Snapshots of Camille Graham flashed behind my eyes. My breath became ragged, reminiscing on the horrid stench of prison. Then I regrouped, steeled my nerves, and reassured myself that I wasn't in any trouble. Yet.

Skin Deep 3

The conference room door opened behind me. I raised my head from my hands and peered at the U.S. Marshall blocking the doorway. He stepped aside and *she* walked in.

CHAPTER 13

Menelik

Agent Bills returned, just as he promised and this time, he brought the bones with him. With three months to max-out my sentence and live the life I'd always envisioned, karma appeared and set my dreams ablaze.

I had just completed my morning workout, still vibing off the sounds of Sizzla on my smuggled in MP3 player when I heard my name being paged to the control room. Initially I thought it was Lt. Brady beckoning me to come break bread with him, but Brady wasn't scheduled to work. Just as I stowed away my contraband, I turned and bumped into two white shirts, both sergeants.

"Put your hands out," Sergeant Sims said. He was a tall redneck I never got along with.

"What's going on, Sarge?" I asked, stalling for time.

"Put your hands out," he repeated with more bass.

The other white shirt, Sergeant Johnson, tried to ease the situation. "Just put your hands out man, everything good," he claimed.

About five minutes later, I knew he was a liar. I shuffled up front in shackles and saw Agent Bills in body armor with long chains and a smile.

He dangled the chains at me. “Menelik! How are ya, pal? Told you I’d be back.”

He seemed too pleased at my presumed demise. I wanted to shoot him the finger. “What’s going on?” I asked.

“You know what’s going on, cop-killer. Time to pay the piper,” he said.

Once again, they led me upstairs to the Warden’s conference room, but this time it was different. This time I was served with murder warrants along with extradition papers. This time I was forced to look at pictures of Born’s slain body, as well as the police officers. This time Agent Bill’s had his facts straight.

This time I was fucked.

I had to see a judge before they could extradite me back to Jersey, so I had a few days to formulate a plan. Or so I thought.

Bright and early the next morning, they packed me up and transferred me to the federal holding facility in Lexington County. I thought I could play it low key until I spoke with Sophie. I wanted to tell her myself. Didn’t want her to get the wrong impression that I was keeping something from her. But the authorities stole that moment from me also. When they removed me from the van outside, news cameras were already waiting on us with their bright lights flashing. I heard one of them refer to me as a “fugitive cop-killer” and I knew then that my days of obscurity were over. I had been thrust into the national headlines right along with my brother's reckless team of bandits.

The only question was: how far would my name reverberate?

CHAPTER 14

Makeda

"Why did you turn snitch?"

Tiffany was sitting just two feet across from me at the long wooden table. I expected her to look haggard and insecure. Instead, she was stunning! Her hair was shiny, thick, and down to her butt. Skin, flawless. Lips glossier and fuller than I ever remembered. Even dressed down in a blue skirt and white blouse, she still looked like a star. Even with the pearls dangling around her neck, she still was a seductress.

And a snitch.

"Makeda, wake up girl!" Tiffany hissed. "Because I ain't no fucking gangster—and neither are you!"

I shrugged my shoulders. "But still..."

"Still my ass!" She lowered her voice and glanced in the direction of the Marshall posted up outside the closed door. They had allowed Tiffany and I to speak before she took the stand earlier that day. They *made* us talk, really. "Makeda, this is not what we signed on for, Hun. We were supposed to use these niggas to get to the top. That's it! All this prison shit was not included. Remember?"

I slowly nodded as the pact we made resurfaced inside my mind. Even though she had a valid point, it just didn't feel right ratting out a man who gave us so much.

"But Slim was good to you!" I argued.

"And? He was good to his other bitches too. Just like Haile was."

Tiffany caught the frown before I could hide it.

"Bitch, I know you don't think you the only one he had."

To my knowledge I was the only one he had. He couldn't possibly have had time to indulge anyone else. I told her so.

"See?" Tiffany shook her head. "That's what I'm talking about. So damn naïve, Makeda! These are street niggas. They have no loyalty."

I sucked my teeth. "I don't know why you pressing me so hard about turning rat. It's not like they even asked me to testify. It's not like I know anything about Slim's business dealings anyway."

"But they will come at you," Tiffany promised. "After I testify today, they will come at you with the same deal they came at me with. Save yourself or die with them. The first person on the bus gets the best seat."

I swallowed the lump in my throat and looked down at the shiny floor. I knew she spoke truth; I knew it was only a matter of time before my personal titanic sank. Even one of the best attorneys in the nation hinted that Haile's days as a free man were numbered.

"You know I'm right, Makeda," Tiffany insisted. "And I know you want to do what's best for you. You just don't know how to do it. You think it's impossible to get out, but it's not, sister. This isn't the life for you. You've supposed to be a star."

I heard her voice crack. I raised my head to see her tears splashing onto the shiny wooden table.

"Tiff—"

She raised her palm to silence me. "Hear me out," she whispered. "You haven't lost anybody yet, but it's coming. If you stay on this path, it's coming. I. Lost. My. Only. Family. All I have left is you and Jesus. I don't want to lose you too, sister. I don't want to lose you too."

I broke down in tears. Powerful sobs that wreaked my body and purged my soul. I reached across the table and embraced my sister. No, I didn't agree with her testifying, but I understood her reasons now.

Tiffany pushed me back and gazed at me lustfully. "I wish I could taste you right now for old time's sake. Remember that time?"

How could I forget it? The freedom, the energy, the passion, the climax. How could I forget it?

"Yeah, I remember," I told her. Suddenly, she grew quiet. Her mood shifted.

"Umm, there's something else I need to tell you also," she said.

Something told me there was some bullshit coming. "Go ahead."

"I'm only telling you this for two reasons. One, it may come out in court. Two, because I think you should know who you're protecting."

"What are you talking about? I'm not protecting anyone!"

Tiffany closed her eyes and nodded slowly. "Yes, you are, Keda. Yes, you are," she whispered. Then she took a deep breath and revealed a skeleton I never expected. "I fucked him."

"Who?" I replied, even though I already knew. "You fucked who?"

"H," she admitted. "First time, him and Slim had a threesome with me. Then, the next time, me and him split this chick that used to dance at Magic City. He was fuckin' her. I was fuckin' her. So, we just fucked her together a couple times."

"Wow..." I pushed back from the table. Stood up. Took a few steps toward the door before the flashes of anger betrayed me.

"How do you think I feel?" Tiffany called from the table. "That little boy he killed and put on that Christmas tree? That was actually my son."

"Whoa!"

I knew she had some bombs to drop but I didn't know she rested on a minefield. Her admissions stunned me into silence.

A few hours after we concluded our talk, Tiffany took the stand in her pretty outfit. Not a man with a dick between his legs could tear his eyes away from her. The women either wanted to be her or hated her because they couldn't. Everybody sympathized with her.

The way she told her story you would've thought she was kin to Virgin Mary and Slim was Satan. I was there when they met, and she had me second guessing whether she was a thirsty stripper on a come up or a victim of riches and charm.

Poor Slim, his face began to crack the moment she took the stand. By the end of day one, I could've sworn I saw a tear gather in his eye. All the arrogance in the world couldn't hide his pain. Just before we took recess for the day, Slim finally lost his cool.

"You dirty broad! This how you do me?" He yelled at Tiffany. He stood up and was immediately tackled by a slew of U.S. Marshalls. "I took care of you! I made you a star! This how you do me?!" He cried from beneath the pile of Marshalls. Dr. Shabazz and Theron dropped their heads in disgust.

Unable to stomach the treason any longer, I stood to leave. I couldn't have known I was heading right into a storm.

CHAPTER 15

Makeda

The next day I woke up in our mini-mansion ready to make the trek back to court to watch Tiffany's treason campaign. No matter how hard I moved, I couldn't get up. Felt like something was riding me. Haile, on the other hand, had been up since the crack of dawn. Working out in the home gym. Cleaning his weapons and avoiding calls on his cell. After court that day, I had a meeting with a rep from Tyler Perry's studio, and Haile was planning to be in the recording studio all day.

I peeled the damp satin sheet down my body and attempted to get up again. As soon as my feet hit the heated marble floor something on the television caught my eye and threw me back in time.

On the screen, in vivid detail was my old hood in Trenton, New Jersey. A gun battle between police and a man on a motorcycle replayed on the screen. Then a police officer's photo with a date stamp of his life and death flashed on the screen. I found the remote and turned up the volume just in time to hear a reporter announce that Menelik had been extradited back to New Jersey and charged with murder of a police officer as well as an assortment of other heinous crimes. Video from his return played while the reporter spoke. As two FBI agents escorted him into the federal building, Menelik shuffled awkwardly, yet he still managed to appear regal. His head was held high and his jaw was set. A warrior's gleam rested in his eyes as he started at the cameras head-on with no shame or fear.

My heart froze in my chest. Emotion snatched my breath away as old feelings resurfaced. *My Menelik was about to be fighting for his life.* I wondered if Haile knew.

"Haile!!!" I called out. My voice echoed throughout the 7,000 sq. ft. home but no one answered. I searched the house frantically for Haile but there was no sign of him.

Haile was already gone.

***

I arrived at the courthouse, my mind whirring like a money machine. I was a tad bit late, so court had already resumed, and Tiffany was back on the stand weaving her tale. I got Slim's attention to ensure him that Haile still was riding for him.

During the first recess Slim called me over within earshot. "Where's H?" He asked.

"At the studio," I replied.

Slim shook his head. "No. Go get him right now and y'all get ghost."

"Huh? What's up?"

Slim peered around cautiously and drew in closer. “Heard they got a warrant for his arrest. They supposed to be picking him up today.”

“What? That’s impossible!”

He nodded vigorously. “Yes, it is possible.” He jerked his head toward the witness stand to illustrate his point. “I’m good here. So, y’all need to go. Tell H I said it’s time to use the spot. He knows. Now go! Take care of my man.”

I dashed out the courtroom without a second thought. Menelik was already cased in, possibly for life. I didn’t want Haile to share his fate. It dawned on me that both brothers had moved heaven and basked in hell to make my existence on this earth a lot easier. They deserved the best of me. Haile had been my personal savior for as long as I could recall. He deserved that I at least warn him and get him to safety. Then, I could get my career back on track after he was tucked safely away on the private island Slim owned in the Caribbean. Who knows, maybe we could end up back in our homeland, frolicking beneath the Ethiopian sun.

But first I had to get him to safety.

When I arrived at the studio, I saw Haile’s diamond-white Cadillac XLR with the mustard-and-mayo vogue tires parked out front. Haile loved that car! With a Corvette engine and convertible hardtop, it was luxury performance at its finest. Haile had the car souped up and bullet proofed too (as were all 9 of his cars). He usually drove that car when he was in a good mood.

That's how I knew he had no idea about his brother.

I caught Haile just as he was coming out the studio. I parked the Porsche truck just as he was getting into his Cadillac. Just before I could call out to him, all hell broke loose.

Dark-colored sedans and SUV's converged on the parking lot from all angles with their tires screeching to a halt. Before they could exit their vehicles and announce themselves, Haile's team opened fire on them with automatic assault rifles. From behind the tinted, bulletproof glass of Haile's Porsche, I watched in horror as bodies dropped mercilessly. The O.A.U. was gunning hard as if they were a special ops team protecting their president. The authorities retreated to the safety of their vehicles while the O.A.U. issued a relentless assault.

Soon, Atlanta City cops rushed in to bolster the agents' surge and a fierce gun battle erupted in broad daylight between the authorities and the bandits. The O.A.U. fought skillfully and valiantly, taking down numerous agents while taking a few loses of their own, and I had a front row seat to it all. It was as if I was part of an action flick. The loud shots seemed to rock the ground beneath the truck as I hunkered down in the leather seat, too nosy to not look and too anxious to regard my own safety.

The tide suddenly turned in favor of the O.A.U. A couple of them rammed their way out of the parking lot in their SUV's while the remaining members retreated inside the studio to safety. I cheered them on as it looked as if they were going to win the battle.

Then the S.W.A.T. vehicle arrived.

Agents poured from the back of the armored vehicle in a single file formation, strategically placing shots at the remaining five or so warriors shooting it out on the sidewalk. Bullets whizzed by them and sparks of fire ripped chunks of bricks from the building. The second volley of shots found their mark and suddenly, bodies dropped like they were being zapped by bolts of lightning, courtesy of the sniper teams on the roof, no doubt. One by one, the O.A.U. members toppled like dominoes. No sooner than their bodies dropped, agents ran up, stood over them, and put two shots in their heads. Once these threats were terminated, they advanced toward the building. The way they were coming I feared for Haile's safety. They had brought the whole calvary along to arrest him and judging from the way they slaughtered the other members of the team, they didn't care if they took him dead or alive.

Just as the S.W.A.T. team made it to the door of the studio, Haile's XLR roared to life from the edge of the parking lot. All eyes whipped in the direction of the coupe to see it peeling out in a cloud of smoke. I wasn't sure if it was Haile inside or not, but whoever it was, I was rooting for them.

CHAPTER 16

Makeda

Hours after the raid I sat inside the interrogation room. After they took out the remaining O.A.U. inside the studio, they secured the perimeter and cleared the area. That's when they found me cowering inside the truck. They cuffed me just like I was one of the crew and stuffed me in the back of an SUV. The way they manhandled me and tossed me around brought back memories I had long suppressed. Echoes of my babies' cries rang out inside my head. This was a real déjà vu moment and I was reliving my past in real time. The interrogation room, the threat of losing my freedom, my career in the balance. As far I'd gone, I hadn't gone anywhere, I realized. It seemed that I always came back to the same predicament; loving the wrong man always seemed to precipitate my downfall.

The agents knew me by name and seemed excited that they had apprehended me. An agent walked in and snatched me from my thoughts. He introduced himself as Agent Rosetti.

"Makeda Barnes?" he asked, even though he held a folder in my hand that probably told my life story.

I nodded. “Could you take these cuffs off please?”

“Suuure,” he cooed as if he was my friend rather than foe. He unfastened the restraints then took a seat across from me at the small table. “So, you wanna tell me about your boyfriend, the infamous H?” He waved his hands and made a spooky sound like a ghost.

I shrugged. “Not much to say.”

“Really?”

I shook my head. “Nope. Unless you know something I don’t.”

He chuckled. “Do I? Of course, I do! For starters, he was the muscle behind Lajuan Singleton’s drug empire. Over the past few years he has committed more murders than Sammy the Bull and Jeffrey Dahmer combined. And you wanna know the best part?”

“I’m listening.”

“He killed your ex-fiancé while you watched.

“Ha! Yeah right!” I shrugged and shook my head vigorously. “Like I said, I don’t know anything about that, sir. Maybe you should go talk to H about that.”

I knew how the game was played. Been there, done that. If they knew so much, they would’ve arrested me a long time ago.

“Oh, we’re going to speak to H,” he assured me. “As soon as he wakes up.”

“Wakes up?” The words tumbled from my mouth before I could stop them.

“Wait, you don’t know?”

“Know what?”

"About H," Agent Rosetti replied. "He crashed his sports car trying to get away from us, shot two federal agents in the process. His car flipped about 20 times while he was in it. He's in a coma right now, but even if he lives, he's still a dead man."

Even though my mind told me he could possibly be bluffing, my heart ruled over my emotions. Just the thought that Haile could be dead buckled me. Before I could gather myself, tears streamed down my face like liquid banners.

Agent Rosetti swooped down to seize the moment of weakness. "It's okay, Makeda. Let it out," he whispered, rubbing my back. "I know it's a lot coming at you right now but now you have to start thinking about yourself Makeda. H can't harm you anymore; you have no reason to be afraid of him. He's done a lot of harm to a lot of people but not anymore." He shook his head. "Not anymore."

While I purged my soul, my mind was still whirring, processing fact from fiction, weighing options, ascertaining the pros and cons of my predicament. Meanwhile, Agent Rosetti continued his quest to flip me.

"This can go two ways for you, Makeda. Real good or really bad. Now, H is going down with or without your help. Either you're gonna sink with him or you're gonna be saved on this life raft I'm offering."

He said the words raft and I thought about the Titanic again. The only few that survived was because of the life rafts they fought over.

Everyone else perished. I didn't want to sink, but I didn't want to roll over either. Still, there were too many variables I was missing.

What happened to H? How was Slim's trial going? Did all the O.A.U. perish? Too many pieces of the puzzle were missing for me to produce a pretty picture.

"Am I under arrest?" I inquired.

"You're in custody."

"So, does this mean I'm under arrest?"

"You're in custody."

"Well, unless I'm under arrest, I'd like to go now please." I had to get out of here, get some air, gain perspective, and check on H.

Agent Rosetti stood to all his six-feet-four inches, crossed his arms, and looked down on me. "Makeda," he said.

"Can I go?"

"Makeda."

The door to the interrogation room creaked open and I knew his reinforcements were coming. I didn't even look back. I just braced myself for the onslaught.

"Is she under arrest sir?" I heard someone ask. I slowly turned over and the first thing I saw was a blue tailored suit. Maybe it was in my head, but he had a glow hovering around him, like he was my guardian angel.

"And who are you, busting in my goddamn interrogation room?" Agent Rosetti barked.

Theron smile and extended a glossy black and gold business card. "I'm attorney Theron Shields.

I represent Ms. Barnes here and unless, she is under arrest, we'll be leaving now."

Agent Rosetti's tan skin blushed red as he threw his hands up in exasperation. "She can go but we will be in touch."

"We'll be waiting," Theron said.

As soon as we settled into Theron's Bentley GT, I breathed a sigh of relief. "Thank you for coming to my rescue," I said.

I noticed he had come alone, the usual entourage from the team absent. I didn't know if that was good or bad.

"Don't thank me yet. This thing is far from over and you're far from rescued."

I nodded. "Guess you're right," I admitted staring through the darkened glass. "What's going on? What happened?"

Theron told me that Haile had taken the Feds on a high-speed chase through the city in his Cadillac XLR. He had eluded them a few times but couldn't outrun the helicopters. They finally managed to cut him off and T-boned his car with one of their trucks. The car flipped 14 times. Wounded and woozy, H still popped out the car, busting. He shot two federal agents before they cornered him off. They engaged in a gun battle right on the side of I-285 before Haile collapsed into unconsciousness from the effects of the injuries he sustained in the car crash. He was cuffed and rushed to the hospital where they placed him in a medically induced coma to stop the swelling on his brain.

As for the O.A.U., every one of them that was there that day was killed. Some from gunshots, others died in the fire when the F.B.I. set the studio ablaze. Over 20 loyal soldiers killed.

"And how is Slim's trial going?" I inquired.

Theron shook his head. "Hard to tell right now. We had the momentum but since his woman took the stand, it doesn't look good. She's killing him. She even brought your name up."

"Really?"

Theron nodded. "She cranked that bus up and rolling over everybody."

"Hmp," I muttered.

Theron merged onto the I-285 loop. I knew he was taking me home then. He had been silent for a few minutes, obviously deep in thought, while a Jagged Edge track hummed low through the speakers. Theron's expensive cologne tickled my senses and the honey-hued leather cupped me inside its softness. It was the most comfortable I felt in a long time.

"Why are you protecting H?" Theron posed. "It's obvious that if you say the right words to the right people, he would be gone."

I shrugged my shoulders and answered honestly. "Guess I never really thought of it as protecting him. I just never had the incentive to think about it I guess."

We pulled through the gates of our home. It wasn't exactly a palace, but it was big enough to be luxurious. I'd picked it out and decorated it all the way down to the marble floors. My own personal castle. Now it felt like I was entering a dungeon, all alone for the night inside 7,000 square feet of opportunity.

Theron drew the Bentley to a halt right in front of my door and I reached for the handle.

"Makeda," Theron called out. "Your career and your future are all the incentive you need to do the right thing. You need to think about that. Few people get a second chance in this world."

"I know," I admitted, and opened the car door.

"Whatever you decide to do, I'll help you."

"Thank you, Theron, it means a lot to me."

I bid Theron farewell and slowly took the trek up the granite staircase preparing to spend my night alone. As soon, I opened the door I realized I wouldn't be alone after all.

Someone was inside, waiting on me...

CHAPTER 17

Makeda

My visitor had been like a sister at one point. We had even been lovers on an occasion. A natural seductress, she wasn't bashful at all about sharing her thick frame, or her skills as a lover. She used to be my best friend, the one I shared everything with. We shared clothes, cars, living spaces, secrets, everything. We even shared my man before, gave him the experience of a lifetime for his 21st birthday.

Now it appeared she was sharing his DNA.

Sophie stood tall to greet me as I walked into my home. Her belly looked as if she was due to go into labor within the hour. Even the colorful, puffy floor-length mink she wore over a goddess dress couldn't hide her stomach. She had the pregnant glow that I imagined was totally opposite from my haggard energy. Her long blond hair seemed extra full, like she was wearing the weave that cost a thousand dollars a bundle.

"Hello Makeda," Sophie said. Her accent was strong and thick, a tell-tale sign that all wasn't as rosy as it appeared.

"What are you doing in here?" I demanded. I'd gone through hell the past few days. I wasn't in the mood for games.

Sophie took a few steps forward. The lone beacon of light downstairs beamed on her like a spotlight. "My husband sent me," she revealed.

"Menelik?" Even though I kinda knew, I still had to hear her say it.

She nodded. "Yeah, he sent me to check on his brother."

I pursed my lips, stunned that the farce was now over. "So, you know?" I asked.

"About them being twins?" She clarified. "He told me just recently. Said he wanted me to know everything just in case he never make it out of that place."

I thought about what I'd saw on the news the morning of Haile's arrest. I initially thought it was awkward that they both were snatched up at the same time.

"How is he?" I asked.

Sophie shook her head. "Not good. There's swelling on his brain, and even if he pulls through, they're saying he may be crippled."

"I was talking about Menelik."

"Oh."

I watched her face contort into a mask of confusion, sorrow, regret, and jealousy in the blink of the eye. For some reason, I felt awkward inquiring about my first love— her husband. But he was *my* first love and I deserved to know if he was okay.

"He's ... he's ... he's going to be okay. Yeah, he's going to be okay," she replied, blinking away tears.

I could understand her wanting to remain optimistic and all, wanting to keep a brave face, but I remembered the furor surrounding that cop's murder. I also recalled Born's assassination. According to the news, Menelik was being charged with both murders and a litany of other charges. From the sound of things, he was anything but okay.

"Where is he?" I asked. "Back in Jersey?"

"No. He's still in South Carolina, awaiting extradition."

We remained standing in silence while a few awkward seconds slipped by. Here we were, two beautiful, successful, ambitious women, tethered to heartbreak by the men we loved.

I motioned to her protruding belly. "How many months are you?"

"I'm due next month." She shrugged, "Twins."

Wow. Twins. For a moment—just a second, I allowed myself to mourn over my babies. Then my humanity kicked in and I offered Sophie a seat. She peeled off her fur and settled into the high-backed black suede chair and told me about the visit with Haile.

According to Sophie, Haile was done. Even if he did survive his injuries, he would never be a free man again. She said it seemed like every alphabet agency in the world had a rep eagerly standing by waiting for Haile to regain consciousness. ATF, FBI, D.E.A, I.C.E., and

Interpol. Even Homeland Security wanted to take a crack at him. He was more heavily guarded than the President of the United States.

Sophie allowed the depth of her report to sink in for a few minutes, then she changed the subject and told me about her and Menelik's company, ARME.

Sophie gloated that their company was flourishing. Seemed Menelik had become quite the businessman while he was away. Sophie swore that Menelik's guidance is what helped them succeed. She was merely executing orders, she claimed. Menelik had also become very wealthy while he was away. Unfortunately, it appeared he would never get to enjoy it.

Or would he?

The more Sophie spoke, the more an idea began to materialize in my head. The solution had been there all along. I just never realized it because I never considered it as an option. The answer had been spelled out for me a long time ago, I was just too blinded by stubbornness to read the letters on the wall. There was one common denominator that could alleviate this bottleneck life. One person that, if sacrificed, could allow everyone else to live. Although the idea was unconscionable before, it was a no-brainer at this point.

"What kind of evidence they have against Menelik?" I asked.

Sophie shook her head and tears began to pool in the corners of her eyes. "I don't know yet. No one is saying anything. He only had a couple more months to go though, and he was coming home to us."

I felt her pain. The pain of losing the love of your life. Forever. I'd felt that same pain. In fact, I was feeling her pain now. I'd never gotten over Menelik. He was, and has always been, my first love. He was in prison because of me. If he had not manned up and come to my rescue, then they would have never been able to capture him. So Menelik was basically facing the death penalty because of me. I felt compelled to do something to help him.

Then there was my impending doom. In all likelihood, my arrest was imminent. The authorities were knocking over all the dominoes in Slim's game. And with Tiffany on the stand singing treason, there was no telling what type of charges they were looking to hang on my head. I was probably about to be taken on another rollercoaster ride with the ending far more severe than my previous stint. And for what? A street administration on the verge of impeachment? I shuddered at the thought.

I cast my eyes toward my one-time best friend and bared my truth. "You know, I think it's fucked up how you went behind my back and stole my man."

"Makeda, it wasn't like that. It just sort of happened."

"Don't know what I was thinking anyway sending you to see my man while he was locked up. Shit, I know firsthand how lonely it can be.

He probably got caught up in the visits. But *you* should've been a better friend."

Sophie dropped her head. "I know, you're right," she admitted. "But *you* should've been a better girlfriend. I just fell in love with him, you know." She raised her head and looked me square in the eye. "And he loves me too."

That was bold. I wanted to smack her for backstabbing me, then having the audacity to justify it. But another part of me felt sad for her and her twins. That was the part of me compelling me forward to take action. That, and Menelik.

Menelik deserved another chance. From what Sophie told me. Menelik had finally evolved into the man I knew he could be. He deserved to give life a shot as that person. The fact that my decision would also grant me another life was the icing on the cake.

"Well, maybe Menelik will have another chance to show you his love, after all." I said.

Sophie looked up. "What do you mean?"

I fumbled around in my jean pocket for a business card. I smiled when I found it. "Let's just say, I have a plan."

THE PRESENT

CHAPTER 18

Menelik

I dip in and out of traffic to find an opening, then accelerate my Aston Martin DBS to 130 miles per hour. I begin rapidly flashing my headlights as soon as I spot a spec of a vehicle about a mile ahead. As is custom over here, the car eases to the middle lane of the Autobahn and I floor it. The engine roars to life in front of me. A gust of air rushes in through the vents in the dash and blows the strong smell of leather around inside the cockpit.

140.

150.

160.

I'm doing 170 before the machine even begins to breathe hard.

I'm on the A6 Autobahn headed to Frankfurt for an arms show. All the heavy buyers and dealers are expected to be on hand. A potentially lucrative trade show to increase ARME's market share.

Since my release from prison a couple of years ago, I've increased ARME's market share to a little over 4%. Sounds like a paltry number, but in a multibillion-dollar industry, that little percentage has us living lovely. We have houses in Germany, New York City, and Charlotte, and a cottage in the Bahamas. I'm getting a home built in Egypt as well as soon as the economy stabilizes over there.

I slow down to make my exit. Just as I ease onto the exit ramp, I see a huge billboard with my beautiful wife smiling over the highway. What she is advertising is insignificant. The billboard is really about Germany's hero remaining on the eyes and mind of its people. My wife has become an icon in her native country, known by just one name.

Sophie.

On the billboard her hair is still as blond as ever, her eyes grey and vibrant. Her natural olive skin glows on the sign. Ample curves from her size-10 frame bust through the wood and desire settles into my loins. Even after giving birth to our twins, she is still the most beautiful woman in the world, not only to me, but to the voters of People Magazine also. As I whiz by her picture, a warm feeling cascades over my body. I speed up, eager to join my wife awaiting me at the arms show.

***

An hour later, Sophie and I are breezing through a room full of the world's rich, ruthless elite in our finest clothes. I'm wearing a black tuxedo with a red bowtie. My wife? She looks stunning in a deep red satin dress. Her hair is swept up on one side, then descending down her right shoulder. We sift through the crowd, sipping rich champagne from glasses with long stems.

Out of instinct, I survey the crowd for threats. Just like old times, my blade is strapped to my wrist beneath my expensive jacket. Guess old habits die hard. It is highly unlikely anybody would bring problems to this crowd. Some of the most dangerous people alive are in attendance. Mexican cartel bosses. Saudi princes. Russian gangsters. Italian Mafioso. Irish freedom fighters. Muslim jihadists. Every faction that has a cause, or something to protect have come out to get a glimpse of the world's latest death makers.

I excuse myself to use the bathroom when I hear someone call out my name.

"Man-ah-lik," the voice yells. I turn to see a blast from my past hurrying in my direction. *It can't be him*, I think to myself.

"Menelik? Is that you, blood?" His rough British accent dispels any doubt. It is him, Don Don, our first mentor into a life of crime.

"Don Don!" I cry out, beaming from ear to ear.

Don Don rushes to me and slams me into a tight hug. "Blood! I thought that wa' you. Look at ya, eh, all dressed up looking like a rich bloke." Don Don jokes as he fingers the satin lapels on my tux.

"You don't seem to be starving yourself," I note. Don Don is about 5' 9" now with deep brown skin and a low haircut. A jagged scar runs from his ear to his mouth, which he subconsciously fingers every few seconds. I imagine it's a reminder of some violent encounter he instigated over the years. Don Don was a terrorist with a knife when we were younger. In fact, he had been our inspiration. It is obvious that he has elevated now though.

"So, what are you doing here, blood?" Don Don asks as he motions to a burly guy behind him to stand down.

"Business," I reply. "I own an arms company, ARME."

"Get out! *You* own ARME?"

I nod with pride. "Yes! Along with my wife." I motion toward Sophie working the room.

Don Don is shocked. His eyebrows raise as recognition sinks in. "Sophie is your wife?"

"Oh, so you heard of her?" I ask, with fake modesty. Of course, he has; everyone has heard of her!

"Heard of her? Blood everybody knows her!"

"Yeah, that's my wife," I confirm.

"So, what are you doing here?" I inquire, eager to change the subject.

Now it's his turn to beam with pride. "I am an arms dealer," he tells me. "I supply arms to the IRA, jihadists, and anybody else with an axe to grind." He shrugs nonchalantly. "No biggie to me. All of their money is welcomed at my bank."

Don Don and I walk out onto the terrace. The convention is being held inside a castle. (In Europe, castles from the old world were converted into living spaces or convention halls). We both accept a drink from a tuxedo clad waiter and stare out into the city while our thoughts congeal.

"What ever happened to your brother, Blood?" Don Don asks. "I saw that he was in a whole heap of trouble some years back. Made it across the pond, so I knew it was serious."

I shudder as that sad fate ripples through my brain. Haile is set to die. He is being executed by the federal government. His crimes were so heinous, they deemed him unfit to roam amongst the living. A serial killer. A mass murderer. A monster. A terrorist. They called him every slur known to man at his plea hearing and trial. He only went to trial for one murder. Did it so they could justify sentencing him to death. He plead guilty to over 50 murders, including the cop I killed that day in Trenton, N.J. He plead guilty to that murder so I could go free.

He exchanged his life for my freedom, the ultimate sacrifice.

I tell Don Don, "He's set to be executed next year."

"Wow!" Don Don shakes his head. "So, the model bitch did him in, eh?"

I nod grimly. "Yep. That she did."

Makeda turned on Haile when he was in the hospital. Everyone thought he was going to die from his injuries sustained in the car crash, so they rushed to paint him as the scapegoat. Makeda debriefed and told them everything she knew. She personally pinned 12 murders on him. By the time he regained consciousness, he was in custody, charged with multiple murders, and she was on her way to a Tyler Perry move set. She may have starred in Tyler Perry's production that day, but *her* story is still being written.

"Doesn't matter though," I tell Don Don. "Haile would rather die than to live life as a paraplegic anyway. So, really he still getting over on them."

Yep. The accident paralyzed Haile from the neck down, which is another reason why he was so eager to fall on the death penalty. He even waived all his appeals so they could execute him faster. The way he saw it, he was still dying a soldier's death. No bending, no breaking. Going out on his shield.

The information leaves Don Don speechless. He tries to put on a brave face, but I can tell the news has him stunned.

"What was Blood thinking, shooting a cop in broad daylight like that?" Don Don wonders aloud as he shakes his head. "I've clipped a few authorities in my day as well, but they were all crooked." He shakes his head at the thought again.

Guilt rises from my belly to my throat and leaks out inside my words. "Sometimes you have to do what you have to do in the heat of the moment," I say, defending my actions more than Haile's.

"But Blood, a cop?" Don Don insists. "All outlaws know they're off limits unless you absolutely have to do them in. Then, in that case you plan it out carefully. Blood, went out Kamikaze style!"

Again, Don Don's words give me pause and force me to lament my decision again, a decision made in the haste of youthful arrogance that sent echoes of disaster well into my adulthood.

Suddenly Don Don turns serious. He rubs the scar on his face and says to me. "You know, I had love for the two of you like my little brothers," he claims. "You see this scar? You know how I got it?"

"I can imagine," I chuckle.

"Can you really, Blood?" His eyes narrow and cubes inside his cognac rattle slightly. "Do you really want to know how I got this scar?"

"I'm listening..."

Don Don finishes off his cognac and leans his back against the railing as he drifts off down memory lane.

"Your mum."

He says the word and I freeze. "What about my mother?"

Don Don nods his head. "Remember that thing that happened to her, and your house maid?"

That *thing* was her death. My mother and our housemaid, Dele, had been brutally murdered while we were living in London. Haile and I came home to find them choking on their own blood. No one was ever fingered for the murders. We assumed that people from our homeland had tracked us down and claimed their retribution.

"Of course, I remember," I tell Don Don.

"Well, I tracked down the braggart that did that to them. Tortured him until he told me why he did it. He caught a lucky break and cut me before I took him out." He rubs the scar.

"What was the reason?" I asked.

"Same reason we're in this bloody business. Money. Your housemaid was bragging that you all were Ethiopian royalty. Some local tough decided to investigate further. Got mad when nothing was in your flat." Don Don shrugs. "The rest is history."

A silence envelops us as his confession takes root. In my mind, I relive that horrific day all over again. The stench of blood is suddenly on the balcony with us. I quickly shake my head and dismiss the vision.

I reach over to hug Don Don like I would hug my brother. Don Don... our first mentor. A big brother... one of the last men on earth I still consider a friend.

Someone walks out onto the terrace. Out of an outlaw's instinct, we both flinch and face the person intruding on our bromance.

"Hey honey, I was wondering where you drifted off to," Sophie says.

She has a stunningly beautiful woman in tow with her. The woman has on a long black satin dress that clings to her slim, curvy body. A split runs from her ankle to the middle of her thighs. Large nipples pierce the thin fabric of the dress and the aura of sex oozes from her. Judging by her olive complexion, I guess she is Italian, although in Europe one could never be certain.

Sophie presents her to me. "This is Fabiana. She is from Naples and is here with a potential buyer from her country." Sophie shoots me a wink. "I thought you may like her."

My wife's comment is really a request for my approval. She is curious to know if Fabiana meets my approval to share our bed. Sophie has always been attracted to women. Years ago, she confided in me that she had been raped by her father from the time she was five until she fled home at 13 to model. The experience turned her against men until she encountered me. Rather than attempt to curb her desire for women, I accepted it and embraced her lifestyle, just as she accepted my past and my faults. Besides, I also get to reap the benefits of her dalliances with women.

"She is gorgeous," I tell Sophie.

She smiles triumphantly. "I thought you might approve." She winks at me and returns inside with Fabiana in tow.

Once we're alone, Don Don raises his glass in a toast. "To the good life, Blood."

I clink my glass with his. "To the good life, Blood."

We toss back our drinks and peer out into the night sky.

"I'm sorry about our brother," he whispers.

"No worries. All violations will be checked. She won't get to see his execution date," I assure him.

Don Don smiles, "I guess I raised you right after all."

CHAPTER 19

Menelik

Fabiana is even more beautiful naked than with her clothes on. An hour after we leave the party, I sit in my favorite chair watching my wife have her way with the curvy Italian. Sophie has Fabiana spread out on her back with her toned legs split wide open while her tongue jabs in and out of Fabiana's tight hole. Fabiana waves her hand in her face as pleasure rips through her body. She mumbles erotic words in Italian as her eyes flutter rapidly. The soft lighting from the running lights on our bedroom ceiling cast an angelic glow on Fabiana's face. She raises her head and stares at me while my wife gives her pleasure. A wave tugs at her and I can see her almost lose her breath. She extends a manicured finger at me and beckons me to her.

"*Venga,*" she says.

The small gesture transports me back in time to Miami. On my 21st birthday Makeda had arranged a threesome for me with Sophie, her best friend at the time. I had been eyeing the thick German for a while. Makeda, being my ride or die at the time, catered to my every fetish, and arranged for me to have her in the context of fidelity. Little did either of them know, I really had needed the stress reliever after the work I'd just put in for my boss, J.L. Gore.

Tomorrow, I am flying back to New York to meet with J.L. Gore to arrange a meeting with my successor in his camp. He is the person who will allow my brother to rest in peace when his number is called.

But tonight, just as it was in Miami, I am accepting my lady's gift.

I stand and walk over to the twisted bodies on the floor. My wife is on her knees tantalizing Fabiana. Her beautiful wide ass is raised in the air and spread open allowing me to see her center glistening with satisfaction. Fabiana raises her head higher and follows my movement. I stand tall behind Sophie, sure that Fabiana can see me. Slowly, I unfasten my trousers. Fabiana's green eyes widen in anticipation. I lock eyes with her as I reach inside my briefs and whip out my erection. Fabiana's eyes grow wider and a smile spreads across her mouth. Slowly I begin to stroke myself as Fabiana watches in amusement. I stroke the entire length of my shaft, then twist and tug at the head. Back and forth I repeat my motions, showing off, enrapturing her with my size.

Sophie becomes aware of me behind her. She raises her ass in the air, jiggles her soft flesh, and beckons me to her triangle of wet heat. I drop down to one knee, my rock inside my hand. Slowly, yet deliberately, I push myself inside of my wife. She arches her back, lifts her head, and exhales a gust of pleasure into the air. Fabiana shudders, her eyes transfixed on my manhood. I burrow my gaze into Fabiana's lustful stare while I bury my flesh inside my wife. Sophie cringes, moans, then releases her orgasm all over my dick. As soon as she gathers herself from the convulsions, she dives her face into Fabiana's vee and sucks on her center as if it's a life source. I feel Sophie's canal warming up, gripping me in a vice. Fabiana's gaze is still locked on me, her eyes pleading for a piece of me while my wife's tongue dances inside of her. I remove myself from Sophie. Her thick juices glisten all over my dick, seeping between the veins.

I stand over Fabiana and kneel. She raises her head to meet me, mouth open wide. I slip the head of my dick inside her mouth. She moans and hums on it as if it's a delicacy. This incites Sophie. She pushes Fabiana's legs up, and really goes hard. As Sophie pushes her tongue deeper inside Fabiana, we turn her into our personal sex toy, sharing our heat with the Italian beauty. She eagerly receives everything we have to offer and shows her gag reflex when I attempt to choke her with my erection.

Sophie stops tasting Fabiana and comes over to me. She gives me her tongue. We both savor Fabiana's taste while Fabiana continues to taste me. Sophie drops to her knees and take my balls into her mouth. She tea bags them while Fabiana sucks me. My knees buckle a bit. I strain to keep from cumming.

"Wait baby," I moan. They both pull on me harder. "Wait a minute!" I demand. I push at

Sophie's forehead and they both release me from their oral clutches. Fabiana's eyes are glazed over as if she just had an orgasm. She lays on her back legs gaped open, gasping for breath. I take the time to really admire the masterpiece of beauty she is from head to toe. Her dark hair is sweaty and matted to her scalp, perfectly arched eyebrows frame smoldering green eyes. A slightly thick, long nose canopies bow-shaped plump lips. A slender neck leads to deceptively large, round breasts with deep brown areoles and deeper brown nipples that are harder than what I'm holding in my hand. Her stomach is flat yet feminine, forming a slightly muscular path to a thin patch of dark hair hovering over thin, glistening pussy lips. Her clitoris is engorged and busting through her lower lips like a starburst. My eyes travel further south and note toned thighs, round calves, and small manicured feet.

Sophie observes me taking all of Fabiana in. "Beautiful, right?" She says. "Go ahead, have her. Have all of her."

I drop to the floor and place Fabiana's legs over my shoulders. She scoots closer to me, eager to reign me in. I guide my dick toward her tight opening and peek inside with the head. Fabiana gasps and tugs at me. I pull her closer to me, drive more of myself inside her. A guttural moan passes through her lips. An expression crawls across her face as if she is being tickled by angels. To our side, Sophie watches the exchange in silence, touching herself.

I plunge deep inside of Fabiana. She wails in agonized pleasure and wrap her arms around my neck. I cradle her knees into my arms, gather her weight, and stand up with my erection still wedged inside of her. She slides all the way down on my dick. Her insides are so hot I nearly spill my seed immediately.

I lift her off me then drop her back down on my pole. She's so tight I barely move inside of her. She feels as tight as a virgin but the way she's savoring the dick tells me she is a seasoned veteran. She rises and falls on me as I thrust upward, impaling her insides with hot lust.

Sophie rises and stands behind Fabiana. She bends down, spread Fabiana's cheeks apart and licks all through the crevices of her beautiful bottom. I fuck Fabiana slower now so Sophie can do her thing back there, and Fabiana loves it! She wraps her arms around my neck and rides me like a mare, her movements more fluid than a ballerina.

Sophie stands, reaches up, and gently pulls Fabiana's head back. Fabiana arches her back and wraps her arms around Sophie's neck. She takes a step back and stretches Fabiana out. Just like that, with Fabiana bridged between us, I lay dick to Fabiana like a madman, hammering her tight pussy, punishing her as if she said something foul about my mother. In my mind she's paying for all the transgressions of the beautiful woman of my past. Each time I jab her insides with my fleshy sword, I am jabbing my blade inside Makeda. My long powerful strokes thrust Fabiana back into Sophie's arms. It's as if we're fighting and I'm trying to knock her out with my dick. The sheer electricity of the moment – me thrusting, Sophie holding her, Fabiana receiving – has me on edge.

I wrap my arms around Fabiana's thighs and slam her onto me. When I feel myself touch the bottom of her gushy vagina, I pause, hold it there, and savor the tight warmth. Sophie clenches her tightly and holds her in place, the three of us frozen in time. Fabiana shudders another climax all over me and I erupt inside of her simultaneously.

Some hours later, Fabiana leaves me and Sophie alone, satisfied in body yet conflicted in mind. Sophie doesn't want me to leave for the States in the morning. She intercepted a call from J.L. Gore and now she thinks I'm back up to my old ways.

If she really knew the nature of my trip, she would abhor me. But it must be done. Business is business.

And I have unfinished business in the States.

CHAPTER 20

Makeda

I couldn't believe my eyes.

I stared through the windshield of the Bimmer, horrified, as the love of my life tried to beat a man to death. Over and over, his mustard-colored Timberland boot crashed into the side of the man's head. Each time the boot connected, the man tumbled over on his back, begging for mercy. But my lover was relentless. No sooner than the man's back touched the wet pavement, that Timberland boot was smashing his midsection, again and again. My man attacked like a shark sensing blood, and the high beams of the BMW shone brightly on the beating, as if this was a stage rather than a rainy back alley, and they were the main stars.

Through the slightly parted window on the passenger side, I heard my man barking out his lines, taunting his prey as he punished him.

"Where is the fucking money, muthafucka?!" ***Stomp!*** *"You think it's a game?!"* ***Stomp!*** *"Got me out here running your ass down in this cold!"* ***Stomp! Stomp! Stomp!*** *The beating was relentless. I'd heard stories about Menelik, how he had transformed from this docile, corny, pretty-boy*

into a beast. I'd even been in the bar the night he leaped into the vaunted ranks of street legends with how he disposed of Born and his brothers.

But to hear of him putting in work and witness him put in work...two different things.

I had to admit though, watching him display his dominance over another man turned me on tremendously. As the vicious beating unfolded right before my eyes, I felt my inner juices percolating until they spilled over and seeped through the side of my panties. I squeezed my thighs together and bit down on my bottom lip, squirming in the leather seat.

For a second, the beating ceased. Menelik stood tall over the man with his hands on his hips, drawing in deep breaths. The man lay on the wet pavement, as still as the concrete. It was hard to tell if he was even still breathing. The heavy rain pelted him mercilessly, and he still didn't move.

Suddenly, Menelik spun and stomped toward the car. Lightning flashed in the sky and lit up his face. In that snippet of light, I saw pure evil in his eyes. He looked nothing like the handsome, charismatic, dapper man I'd grown to know and love. This Menelik was in straight beast mode as he walked past me to the trunk of the car. It appeared that he was possessed by something evil. I felt him fumbling around back there and I silently prayed that the man would just disappear before he found what he was searching for.

But it didn't happen that way.

Menelik found the steel tire jack and quickly returned to his victim, holding the weapon inside his right hand. Unconsciously, I slid down into the seat, afraid of what I was about to witness, yet too nosy to turn away completely.

"So, you don't have the money?" I heard Menelik ask. The answer must have been no, because Menelik raised the jack handle high in the air and brought it crashing down on the man's skull. A burst of thick blood ejected from the man's head onto Menelik's Timberland boot. I bit down on my hand to stifle my scream. Felt like my meal from earlier was threatening to reappear in my lap. My whole face blushed warm with fear, and my heart began galloping wildly inside my chest. The scene that had incited me to pleasure just seconds ago now had me blooming in fear.

I glimpsed the clock on the dashboard. It read 10:30. I was due at the afterparty for the fashion show no later than 11:00, and here I was cutting the clock, flirting with danger. Depending on the traffic, it would take us at least an hour and a half to get back into the city. Why, oh why, did I have to ride back into Jersey with this fool?

Menelik turned the man over on his back and plundered through his pockets until he discovered a small knot of money. He rifled through the bills, took what was his, and tossed the remaining bills onto the man's chest. Then he calmly walked over to my side of the car and tapped on the window.

I rolled the window down halfway and drops of rain drifted into the car. "Yeah?"

He wiped a light sheen of rain from his forehead with the sleeve of his Carhart sweater.

"Turn the car around and wait for me at the edge of the street," he instructed.

"But Menelik – "

"No buts, Makeda. Do it now. And turn the music up a little bit."

I wanted to remind him of the time, and what was important in our lives, but it would've been futile. When he was in this mode, he only understood one thing. His objective. So, I did as I was instructed, turned the car around and waited on him at the edge of the alley.

I knew the real reason he wanted me to turn the car around was to shield me from the most horrific part of what he had to do to get his dollars, but I couldn't stop myself from staring out that back window. I cringed as I witnessed Menelik's silhouette rain down blows on the man's head with the jack handle. He was cutting into him so deep that I saw shadows of blood (or maybe brain matter) leaping into the air. The man maneuvered himself into a fetal position, but Menelik was relentless with that jack handle. He pummeled him mercilessly as I watched on in a mixture of fear and excitement. I couldn't deny that as horrified as I was, I was also getting aroused.

Thankfully, the beating was over just as quickly as it began. Menelik returned to the car and tossed the bloody jack handle into the trunk. Then he settled into the passenger's seat and stared ahead into the rainy night while I drove off, headed into the city. Currents of suffocating energy wafted from his body and permeated the car as his chest heaved up and down rapidly. He shifted his body in the seat until he was comfortable, peeled off his black leather gloves, and unrolled the bundle of money he had taken from the man. My eyes quickly darted from the road to the money. Seems like a little bit of money for so much violence, I thought to myself. Then again, the price of a life always went cheap in the streets.

Menelik quickly tallied up the money, then counted it again, clearly displeased with the results. He sighed loud enough to rattle me. "I gotta go back by your place," he whispered, never taking his eyes off the bloody stack of bills.

"But baby, I'm already late for the party now. Devin has already warned us that every girl representing D.A.M.E. had to be there," I reminded him. "I can't miss this."

He mulled my words over in silence for a few seconds, chewing on his jaw so hard I'm sure he tasted blood.

"Makeda," he whispered. "I know how important this modeling thing is to you, but I have to make sure this business is taken care of first."

I transferred my mood to the accelerator of the Bimmer and the car rocketed forward.

"Menelik, even though I don't agree with your lifestyle, I told you I would support you," I reminded him. "But, I need your support too."

He waved the stack of bills in my face. "And I am supporting you, with this right here. You not a superstar yet."

"And I will never be one at this rate."

He sighed and took his attention away from the money for a second. "Okay look," he said. "just drop me off at your spot in the city and you go on to your party. If I finish in time, I'll meet you there and we can have a good time. Fair enough?"

He stroked my leg to make his offer go down smoother, and my insides flared up with passion. He aroused me to infinite heights when he turned from fire to ice in the blink of an eye, and he knew it. I cut my eyes at him seductively and nodded my agreement to his proposal. Menelik tucked the money away and placed his cold, soft hand inside the split in my dress.

"Hmm, your hands are cold," I moaned.

"I know. That's why I'm trying to warm them up." He flashed a devilish smile then slid his hand farther up my thigh.

His finger brushed over the sticky liquid I had released earlier when he was putting in work and he drew in a sharp breath. "Yeeah, that gangsta shit turn you on, don't it?" He said. "You know this gangsta shit go two ways though. If you ever cross me, this gangsta shit will be turned on you, Keda..."

My eyes snap open and instantly I feel the beads of sweat rushing down my face. The silk sheets cling to my naked body and another chill zips through me. I roll out of bed and walk out onto the terrace to clear my head. The cool night air caresses my body and the wind whips my long hair into a frenzy all around me. I stare off into the distance at the sights of New York City several floors below me and attempt to clear my head.

This is the third night in a row that I dreamed of Menelik. In fact, they weren't dreams, they were recollections, and each recollection was a trip down memory lane to the journey of days past.

As a young woman, I had been the very definition of a ride or die chick. I'd witnessed Menelik do harm to more people than Ted Bundy in a more brutal fashion than the history of the United States. Through it all, I kept my cool. Held our secrets on my tongue. Never betrayed his trust. Then at the lowest point in his life I left him for dead in the tombs of the South Carolina Department of Corrections. Now just like the mythical Phoenix, he was back among the living.

In my heart I know it's only a matter of time before Menelik pays me a visit, especially after what I'd done to his twin, Haile. I had crossed two of the most dangerous men I'd ever known, and their inevitable retribution is preventing me from sleeping.

"Hey Babe, what are you doing up?" His deep baritone voice startles me. He wraps his beefy arms around me from behind and I melt into his embrace.

"I can't sleep."

"Again?"

I sigh deeply. "Yeah."

"The dreams again?"

I nod slowly and look up into the stars. "Yep."

Thomas swoops in to whisper in my ear. "Makeda, I'm not going to let anything happen to you, baby. Your past is in the past. I got you now. Those... *niggas* aren't going to do anything to you on my watch."

Thomas attempts to comfort me with his words, but the way he says his words force me to doubt he could really protect me if it ever went down. He even says *nigga* like a cornball. He may be one hell of an attorney, but outside of the courtroom, he is more awkward than a lion in the ocean.

"I know baby, I'm not really worried. The dreams are just so vivid, and ever since my ex came home from prison... I'm a little worried."

Thomas rubs my shoulders, "Relax baby, your ex isn't even in the country right now," he says.

"Huh? How do you know???" That catches me off guard. How does he know Menelik's schedule?

Thomas smiles, "I have my sources," he replies cryptically.

I spin and look up into his hazel eyes. My eyes narrow into optic slits. "What are you not telling me? How do you know where Menelik is?"

Thomas shrugs, "I put my best P.I. on him as soon as you told me he was back on the streets. He went to visit his brother, then he flew to his home in Germany to be with his wife."

The word *wife* curdles my blood every time I hear it, and these days I can't get away from Menelik's wife. She is everywhere. Sophie has become a megastar, an internationally known *slasher.* Model/Actress/Entrepreneur/Producer. The only thing she hasn't done was cut an R&B album, and with an empire estimated to be worth over $70 million, she could probably buy herself a platinum plaque too.

"Trust me baby, I'm on him. He will never do you any harm," Thomas reiterates.

"Thank you, baby," I push a weak smile on my face and offer it to him. He pulls me into his hard body so tight it feels as if our bodies merge as one. I allow myself to get lost in his embrace and attempt to release my concerns into him.

I have been living in a constant state of fear ever since I turned against Haile a couple years ago.

After Sophie came to see me, I had an epiphany the next day. With the S.K.G. in shambles, and the O.A.U. on the brink of extinction, I had no one to hold allegiance to. I realized I was holding on to a code that I never signed up for. I wasn't a hustler, killer, or extortionist. Hell, I wasn't even an outlaw. I was a tax-paying citizen, a former supermodel, a woman on the brink of stardom that could write my own rules and punch my own ticket.

I was also a woman with a debt of regret and a way to erase my bill.

I didn't intend to hurt Haile; that wasn't my initial intent. The way the story came to me, he was a dead man clinging to life already. So, I figured he would condone my decision, figured he would quickly trade his life for his brother's freedom.

So, I did the unthinkable.

I waltzed into court the next day and flipped on Haile. I didn't tell everything I knew. If I had done that, we would have still been in court. Haile had a body count like the National Cemetery in D.C. I couldn't do him *that* dirty. I simply did enough to lock him in and let Menelik out.

I gave them the gift of the identity of the Nimrod murders. And I told them that it was Haile – not Menelik – that killed that police officer in Trenton, New Jersey.

To my surprise, Haile corroborated my story and quickly tried to plead guilty to the Nimrod murders to save his life. The government rejected his plea for the killing of the baby, but they allowed him to admit to taking part in four-dozen other murders.

Then they convicted him and sentenced him to death for killing that baby.

Haile may have been physically handicapped and confined to a box, but his power and influence is stronger than ever. He still has a voice through his old artist, Dirty Red.

Dirty Red has become a rap superstar. Because of the attention the trial garnered, and Dirty Red's affiliation with the gang, he catapulted to super stardom. Seemingly overnight, he became a rap superstar, doing collabs with the likes of Flame and Qwess, and repping the gang harder than ever. He became Haile's personal mouthpiece, memorializing him in his gangsta raps. Haile's conviction confirmed that Dirty Red wasn't just rap capping, so the fans conferred the ultimate stamp of authenticity on him by proxy.

Dirty Red let the whole world know who had betrayed his boss. On wax, he called me out by name, so while I was being celebrated in Hollywood, I was being vilified in *Hollyhood.* He even had a song that mocked a whole story of how the gang hunted me down and pulled my tongue through a slit in my throat for snitching. The song was done to a catchy bounce beat so the deadly implications and misogyny rode beneath the allure of the 808, but the takeaway was that I wasn't shit and that one day I would meet a nasty fate like Tiffany.

But that was another story.

Thomas walks me back inside from the cool night air. He lays me on the bed and massages the tension from my neck. Then he gently lays me back on the satin sheets, ease my legs open, and glide his tongue over my pussy nice and slow. In minutes, I climax with lightning crashing behind my eyes. I'm so terrified that, in my mind, the flashes are from the muzzle of Menelik's gun.

I shudder, shiver, and shake but not from pleasure.

I know Menelik is coming soon, and I am mortified.

CHAPTER 21

Menelik

I can't front. I never thought I would see these gritty streets again outside the memories etched forever in my mind. I had come alive in these gritty streets, turned tragedy into triumph and bossed up on a check. Now I have returned to revel in my splendor.

I click the left paddle and the V12 purring in front of me roars to life. I'm rolling down E. State Street in an Aston Martin the color of dandruff. This isn't the same Aston Martin my wife bought me while I was inside. This is the new number, the flagship, droptop model.

I stop in the middle of the street and activate the hazard lights. Then, I push a button to peel the top back. As the blood red top descends slowly, every eye on the block is fixated on me. I imagine the chrome dipped deep dish rims are blinding them.

I see someone point and I hear them say, "Ohhhh shit! That's the boy..."

"Menelik, right?" Someone adds.

I smile and adjust the Gucci aviator shades hogging my face. Then I slowly pull off with a smirk.

Ever since my brother's trial catapulted us into the national media stratosphere, everyone recognizes me. When Haile lied about murdering that cop, coupled with his treacherous run in Atlanta, he instantly became a street legend. His deeds were the stuff Hollywood movies were made of. (Hell, he even had an offer from Pen 2 Pen Multimedia to turn his story into a film. The head of the company paid him regular visits to capture his story for a book to add to his catalog of Gangsterotica tales.) Haile's admission to being responsible for over 50 murders put him in a league of his own. The U.S. government labeled him a serial killer; the underworld labeled him a legend, larger than life because he begged for the death penalty, unlike the Italian mob rats of yesteryear.

To the streets, Haile had done things the right way. He got money, bust his gun, fucked the baddest bitch in the game, pushed foreigns and exotics, rocked designer – all the things hip-hop artists boasted of doing – and then begged for the death penalty.

Where they do that at???

Haile embodied the best and worst of the streets; I embody the best and worst of Haile. So, since I am free, the streets confer their respect and praise for him upon me. Not to mention the fact, I had gotten down and dirty in this town myself years ago and essentially beat the system.

The same way I lived vicariously through Haile; he is now living vicariously through me.

I chunk the deuces up at the fans pointing at me and rev the engine again to inspire them before I hang a left on a side street.

I pull up to the building that used to be called the Caravan and spot a shiny, black Jaguar XJ idling at the curb. The windows are so dark I can't see inside, despite the sun beaming down on us. I don't need to see inside to know who occupies the vehicle. The lights on the Jaguar flash twice and I pull my Aston up on the driver's side. The window on the Jaguar eases down and I am face to face with my mentor.

"I see you, Superstar!" JL Gore greets me, beaming with pride. "You left the ghetto a fugitive and came back a boss!"

"Ayeee, somebody gotta do it!" I sing.

"I know that's right!" JL says, looking around. "Hop in here with me so we can talk. You can pull your car in there. Ain't nobody gonna bother it."

I park my car in the vacant lot and hop in the passenger seat. As I settle into the warm leather, I have a small flashback of the first time this old timer pulled up on me in Donnelly Homes.

Back then he was pushing a Jaguar too, and so were his brothers that were with him. I thought it was a wrap for me, for everyone in Trenton knew how treacherous the Gore brothers were. They moved like smoke and smothered their opposition in silence. After Haile and I had taken out Born and his brothers, we thought the Gore brothers were the calvary sent to right our wrongs. Instead, JL Gore was pleased with us and offered me a job. The rest is history... or should I say, legend.

"I'm so proud of you for escaping all this bullshit, man. When I heard them pigs had you boxed in down South, I just knew it was over for you, youngblood. They don't play about one of their own."

As he talks, I stare out the window at the dirty city creeping past the window. Trenton looks like an episode of the *Walking Dead*, all zombied out. I didn't think it could get any worse than the ghost town I left behind, but it looks downright apocalyptic now.

"That was a pretty clever move you pulled with your brother," he says. "I should've known it was two of you. The way you handled things so efficiently at times and seemed to be in two places at once. That was genius," he says. "Your moves brought some heat on me. Let me tell you what I've been through..."

JL Gore relays to me that as soon as I left Trenton, the authorities swarmed on him and his brothers. They quickly discovered that JL Gore was connected to us – the cop killers – and brought all their wrath down on them. The cops that JL Gore had on the payroll that had protected him from harm for a dozen years rolled on him. He had to get light and headed for greener pastures down South where I had hidden out before. While he was gone, one of his brothers, Reo, was snatched up by the authorities and sent to the Feds.

While JL was down South, he heard all about the dust being kicked up by the S.K.G. and the O.A.U., and when Slim's empire was toppled and he was sent to the Feds, it just so happened that while Reo was in the Feds, he bumped into members of the gang. By then, the secret was out of the terror we wreaked on the Northeast and the South. Names were dropped, stories were swapped, and the pieces were connected that made them fam by proxy. Next thing you know, Reo was kicking it with the gang inside, not as a sycophant, but as a contemporary. Game recognize game and bosses recognize bosses.

"When does Reo come home?" I ask JL.

"He's already home. We're going to see him now."

We cut a few corners while we continue to make small talk. Then, JL drops into a deeper subject.

"No one could believe that our homegirl flipped on you and your brother like that," JL says. "The city was buzzing about that for quite some time. We hailed her as one of our own, but Trenton don't breed rats."

"Yeah, I know. That shit was crazy!"

"And what the fuck was your brother thinking, admitting to that shit?"

"Well, I guess he figured wasn't no use in both of us being boxed in. Somebody gotta live to tell the story."

JL laughs. "I can dig that shit."

We pull into the driveway of a beautiful home in West Trenton, a stone's throw from where we used to live. JL honks the horn and a few minutes later, a big man lumbers from inside the home. He looks like a bigger, older version of JL, except his skin is two shades lighter. He goes to the back of the Jaguar, and climbs in behind JL. He's so big, I'm surprised he can fit inside.

"What's up, Youngblood?" Reo says to me as he offers his hand.

I accept the handshake. "Hey, O.G., how are you?"

"Great – now that I'm free. I just gave them Pigs almost a nickel, but I'm back stronger than ever."

"You know I can relate."

"I know that's right," Reo says. "But your brother will never see this side of the streets again, unfortunately."

We pause in silence in honor of my brother's struggle.

"It's alright though," Reo says. "Your brother sent me with one last request. Said I have to deliver it to you personally, so I'm glad you came."

Reo lights a stogie as JL eases from the driveway slowly.

"Wouldn't miss this for the world," I say. "So what is it?"

"I'm sure you know already," Reo says. "He's due to be executed next month. He's holding strong to the end in there." He pauses for me to catch his drift. When I leave him hanging, he speaks Haile's final request to me. "He wants you to take care of the girl, the one that did him in."

"Keda?"

Reo nods as if he would be committing a crime to utter a word.

JL looks out the window and blows smoke rings through the open roof.

"I didn't expect this," I admit.

The last time I heard from Haile, he expressed to me that Makeda had done him a favor by ratting him out. I know she definitely did me a solid. If it wasn't for her ratting, I would be rotting. So, I am conflicted in more ways than one. True, she had broken the laws of the jungle, but that is terrain I no longer roam. I am a legal millionaire now; my thought process is different. Although I am sure my company, ARME, is responsible for the deaths of many, it has been years since I participated in a murder directly. Just being around these gangsters has me uneasy.

"Why not?" JL asks. "If someone ratted out my brother, he wouldn't even have to ask me to do something to 'em because I would be too busy doing it."

"You better," Reo confirms.

"You ain't gone Hollywood on us, have you?" JL jokes. "Shit, once upon a time, you would be already doing it too."

I shake my head. "Nah, it's not that. It's just that I have to move carefully. I know them boys on my ass; I can feel the heat on my cheeks. No homo." I chuckle a bit to lighten the mood, but there is no way to lighten the mood of three decades of killers. This luxurious Jaguar might as well be a hearse with all the past death looming inside.

"I always feel like I'm being tracked and shit," I admit.

"You probably are," JL suspects. "You embarrassed them people more than O.J. You killed a cop on video *and* was on *America's Most Wanted.* They ain't never gonna let you live in peace – not in the States, anyway."

"Which is why I got the fuck out of Dodge. But I have to finish my war here first before I can live in peace anywhere..."

Silence envelops us for a beat. Then, JL breaks the thick air.

"So, I know a guy," JL says. "He can take care of this for you. He's a mean motherfucker, international hitman, not no street cat. Very efficient... discreet...specializes in high profile shit like this. But he's very expensive."

"Are you sure he can get it done?" I ask.

"Absolutely."

"Ok then, the money doesn't matter. But... I want to meet him myself. I'll throw you something for turning me on to him too though."

JL waves his hand dismissively. "Don't disrespect me, Youngblood. We're family. When she crossed ya'll, she crossed us too. I do want you to open up the pipeline to those weapons though. Let's do some business with that after this is done."

"Done," I assure him. "So when can I meet this guy?"

"I'll arrange it for you in the next couple of days. When I call, be ready to move."

"Say less."

CHAPTER 22

Makeda

I step foot onto the concrete outside my condominium. The Maybach Mercedes is idling for me at the curb. I look both ways and over my shoulder before I accept the open door the driver holds for me. I climb inside and poke my head around the cabin to make sure the coast is clear inside. I know Menelik is rich and has means to have others do his bidding, so I'm rarely comfortable outside my condominium. With Haile's upcoming execution dominating the news, I can imagine the fresh wounds being rebirthed.

"Everything okay, Ms. Barnes?" The driver asks. "I see you are nervous, but I can assure you, you are safe." He nods to the rearview mirror. "You see that truck behind us? They're the best trained security detail in the city. Relax. This will be the smoothest ride to the radio station ever."

I peek behind us and sure enough, there is a huge, tinted Suburban riding the bumper of the Maybach. I relax and kick my feet up. I pop a Zan-x and focus on the news playing on the television attached to the back seat as we slowly pull off into the Manhattan traffic. The first thing that catches my attention on the television screen is the

Breaking News report. I see a picture of Tiffany flash across the screen and my heart sinks. I turn up the volume to hear the report.

According to the reporter, Tiffany was tracked down and an assassination attempt was made on her life. Someone riddled her SUV with bullets and when she emerged from the vehicle with her young son in tow, only then did they stop. The bandits took her son and left Tiffany on the streets bloody.

I flash back to the last time I heard about Tiffany.

After Tiffany flipped on Slim and the whole S.K.G., she vanished into thin air for nearly a year. When she emerged, she emerged with Slim's baby, heading a new modeling agency she owned. She ran her agency from the shadows of society, only active on social media. Tiffany had developed a cult-like following Slim's trial. It didn't hurt that she was drop-dead gorgeous still. It was rumored she was living in Colombia or the D.R., and with her surgically enhanced body and perfect new smile, it wasn't hard to believe. Her mystique only added to her popularity. She had managed to successfully balance her secret persona with her popularity until now.

I lean back in the seat, sympathetic for Tiffany, but grateful that her plight isn't mine.

***

Menelik

"I want her dead."

As soon as the words escape my mouth, I feel normal again. Back to my former powerful self. Energy surges through my body as the realization of my words take root inside my core. "I don't want this bitch to see the New Year's sun rise on her pretty ass. Got that?"

My passenger shifts in the tan leather passenger seat of my Rolls Royce Wraith, desperately swatting the thick smoke wafting from the end of my joint like people in my homeland swat flies. I retrieve the picture from the inside pocket of my suit jacket and finger it, the grooves still fresh in my hand. The grooves still fresh in my mind. I twist a knob and the starlights burrowed inside the headliner glow a soft light to illuminate the cabin. I pass him the picture.

"Menelik! This is... this is..."

"Problem?" I ask.

He expels the deep breath trapped in his chest. "No problem. It's just that...well, she looks like that woman from T.V., and all those magazines. Makeda Barnes."

If looks could kill, he would be in the Hudson, floating amongst the rest of the sewage.

I snatch the magazine from the backseat. Thumb to page forty-two. Rifle all the way through the spread to page forty-nine. Stuff the book in his lap, on top of the picture. "Look at her gotdamnit! Look at her good, 'cause that's your target, her right there."

Slowly, he flips through the pages. Her sensuous eyes tantalize the camera the same way they used to tease me. Her dangerous curves pop from the pages as if they have a life of their own. Curves I know better than the ridges of my own body. With no shame, she revealed to the world all the blessings the creator has bestowed upon her.

"Wow! She is gorgeous, Menelik."

He is speaking to himself, more than me. I know if I was someone different, someone less dangerous, someone with a more favorable past, he would have a lot more unsavory things to say. Things that would cost him his life if he says them to me. "Look at those eyes," he whispers under his breath. I shift in my seat.

"Damn, only way I'd ever get a woman this fine is with duct tape, a stun gun, and a fast car." He laughs at his own joke. I don't.

My gaze is fixed on the Manhattan skyline across the river. Thoughts on what she is doing permeate my mind. I know she is there. Her itinerary is posted all over her website, and I heard her interview on the radio earlier in the day. It has been a while since I have felt her, but I can still *feel* her.

I inhale a lungful of pungent poison to settle my thoughts. Seldom do I smoke, but I must admit, it keeps my mind clear on those rare occasions my conscience pay me a visit.

"So can you handle this or not?" I ask. He hesitates a little longer than I like. Hesitation is a sign of fear. Fear precedes failure. Or success. Depending on how you use it.

"Well, because she's so famous, it may be a little harder than I first imagined," he reasons.

But I'm not trying to hear it. Excuses repulse me.

"I'll double your pay. Two-hundred K," I offer. "Now can you make it happen? Can you bring me her head so I can put it on my mantle and avenge my brother?"

Again, he hesitates before answering. Finally, "Sure, Menelik."

"Sure? 'Cause if you can't..."

"No, no, I'll make it happen," he assures me. Guess he understands that if he says no, it would be him that would die. Tonight. I was done killing, but...

Reluctantly I smile. "So what time frame are we talking here? I'm serious; I don't want this bitch breathing the New Year air with me."

He waves his hand dismissively. "Don't worry. I got it," he assures me.

I reach beneath the seat. Retrieve a leather briefcase. Black with red, gold, and green piping. I pop it open. One-thousand pictures of Benjamin Franklin greet me. I pass it to him. "Down payment."

He returns the photo and magazine, and then gathers his things. I hit a button and the suicide door slowly glides open. He eases one foot out of the long door, then, as if he can no longer contain his curiosity, he looks at me. For the first time in our encounter, he looks directly at me.

"I gotta know, Menelik," he says. "I-I just have to know. Why? Why kill her?"

"Some things are better left unsaid," I tell him. "But if you must know..."

Flashes of our time together careen through my head like a highlight reel. The Good. The Bad. The Ugly. The Grind. The Climb. The Time. The Disappointment. The Reconciliation. The Betrayal. Our story read like a bestseller. We lived a life made for Hollywood. More like Holly*hood;* too real to be scripted.

But it was our story

I look at him and answer the question that had been gnawing at me as well. "Because I love her."

He pauses for a brief moment. "You guys sure have a funny way of showing love in this country," he says. "In my country, when we love a woman, we grab her and cherish her. Show her a love like no other man has ever shown."

I take in his words and raise him one. "How do you handle betrayal in your country?" I ask.

Without hesitation, he replies, "Death. Treason is punishable by death."

"Exactly. Let me know when you have completed the job."

CHAPTER 23

Makeda

"Move, and I'll shoot." I hear the voice but I can't see who is speaking. The red beam from the object he clutches in his hands is blinding me. "I mean it. Move, and I'll shoot," he repeats.

My heart thumps with excitement. My mouth goes bone dry. I freeze harder than ice cubes in sub-zero temps. Slowly, I rise on my toes and lift my arms to the lights. Immediately, the cool air drifting through the open window chills my body. My large brown nipples harden in protest and wink at him from beneath my thin tank top.

Suddenly, a thin smile spreads across his face. He motions at my shirt. "Take it off. Real slow, take it off. And look at me while you do it," he adds.

I frown my nastiest scowl, but my body refuses to lie for me. I am becoming wetter and wetter by the second, and the dark spot staining my pink, satin, French-cut panties shows him just how aroused I am at his show of force.

He smiles harder. "Yeeeah, I knew you liked this shit." He points the shiny object in his hand at my panties. "Take those shits off too. Let me see that pretty pussy."

Seconds later, I stand before him as naked as the day the doctor snatched me from my Ethiopian mother's womb. Fidgeting from foot to foot, with abated breath I await his next command.

"Lay on your back on the couch," he barks.

I hop my naked ass onto my cold, red leather loveseat that's shaped like lips. Behind me, thirty stories below, the heart of Manhattan screams its existence in an untuned melody of horns, sirens, and music. The sounds that beckoned me to this great city like a promising lover, now only a distant backdrop in my mind. All that mattered was this moment.

"Spread your legs," he says. "Open that muthafucka up. Play with it." I obey his commands. "Yeeeeah... like that... just like that... play with that pretty muthafucka. Don't stop." He aims the metal right between my legs. "Don't stop... keep playing with it."

I dip two fingers inside of my hot, wet center as if my life depend on it. I pull them out. Flash them at him. My thick, creamy juice coat my slender fingers like rich yogurt, sliding down them slow like molasses. My unique scent, a combination of all the fruits I've consumed in the past week, perfume the room like exotic incense. I know he can't resist me much longer. I spot his hardness threatening to burst his olive-colored slacks. I know now, it is time for me to take control of this encounter.

I beckon him to me with sticky fingers. "Come here. Take it out. Let me see it. Come *onnnn*," I urge him.

He hesitates a moment, indecision etched in his dark face. Though in the heat of the moment, I cannot deny he is attractive, more ruggedly handsome than pretty-boy. As if noticing them for the first time, my eyes lock on his full lips. Under different circumstances I would love to kiss them, maybe suckle them for a few extra seconds to revel in the taste. Unfortunately, they are now twisted up into an ugly scowl as if they'd never been kissed before. If I could only get him to smile, I think.

"Come on, take it out," I beg. "Let me see it. I know you want to. It's harder than that thing in your hand. Let me see what you working with."

I can see him contemplating, weighing his options, ticking off the pros and cons. Finally, he arrives at a decision and grips his zipper. Seconds later he releases a monster.

His long, skinny dick unfurls from his pants like Mr. Snuffleupagus, bobbing to its own rhythm. With one hand gripping his metal, and the other hand gripping his meat, he begins to stroke himself. The harder he pulls, the deeper I dig inside my tunnel, totally aware that I have hijacked this scene, totally aware that I have reached the point of no return.

I am about to come.

Moans effortlessly ease through my lips as I release a small river on the loveseat. I raise my toned butt inches from the cushion and hump my bald mound on my hand like a hellion in heat. I feel the familiar tingling sensation rising inside my belly, then crawling down toward my center. A strong current of electricity zaps my core, as a flash of light explodes behind my eyes.

"I'm cumming!!!" I wail in ecstasy. "Sheeeeit, I'm cumming!!!!" Through blurry vision I see him pulling on himself as if he's trying to rip his huge dick from his body. Before I can blink, his semen explodes from the tip and splashes me in the face like hot lava.

Then he pulls the trigger on the metal instrument inside his other hand.

His iPhone flashes multiple times, capturing in vivid detail, my freaky face drenched in his life-fluid. I massage his seeds deep into my skin, reveling in the scent, texture, and feel of his essence becoming one with my skin. I slide my fingers down my throat and taste him, then slowly withdraw them and lick them like a lollipop. I moan so loud it echoes off the walls.

He drops before me on his knees, spread my legs wider, and give me the respect I deserve. He praises me like the Ethiopian goddess I am. I moan to the heavens.

"Yes Thomas... right there... eat this pussy... oh yeah... it's yours, it's yours... damn baby, it's yours!"

Thomas always knows how to please me. He is the only man I've met in this huge, limitless city that is just as freaky as me. Amazing in a city of millions! We always tease ourselves to mutual climax before the real action goes down. After he busts the first time, the man can fuck for hours – especially if he knows I am about to travel out of town for a movie or photo shoot. This personal photo shoot is for his benefit. He says the pics allow him to "work" while I am away. From time to time, I send naked pictures of myself from exotic locales to keep me fresh in his mind, but he says he wanted something more personal this time. Guess there is nothing more personal than the pics he just snapped. He could probably see my heart pulsing through my vagina as wide as I had it split open for him. But if that's what he wants, that's what he receives. I am a loyal, throwback chick, the last of a dying breed. On the surface, I may appear as if I am of the country I reside, but I am Ethiopian to the bone. First-generation American. I live to please my man, and for the past six months, Thomas Addison, Esq. has been mine.

Thomas keeps lapping at me until I can no longer stand it. "Put it in baby," I plead, reaching for his hard dick. "Fuck me, Thomas. Feel your pussy. It's hot and ready for you. Come onnn!" I am practically foaming at the mouth.

"You want this dick?" he asks. I nod so hard I hear bones pop in my neck. "Well, take it then. Put it in your mouth, Keda. Suck it. Suck your dick."

Seconds later, I feel him at the back of my throat, knocking on my tonsil door, begging to slide down into that sacred space. With a slight tilt of my head, I relax my throat and grant him entry into the deep throat club. I hum and fondle his heavy balls just as he prefers while I put forth my best effort to swallow all seven inches he is offering me.

I feel his loins stirring, ready to produce again. For me, seeing his face when he erupts his passion is the highlight of our sexual encounters. I absolutely love to see his hazel eyes roll into the back of his head when he cums!

I look up into his eyes, ready to claim my prize. Instead, I see the shadow of a stranger hovering above his head. Before I can react, a gloved hand loops around my baby's neck and a loud pop echoes throughout my condo. Before I even realize what has occurred, I am swallowing Thomas's final piss.

Choking on my man's final whizz, I fall back onto my chair, looking at the scariest sight I'd ever seen in my life. Thomas's body, so strong just seconds before, is now crumpled on the floor. His head dangles awkwardly on his chest, his neck broken. A tall, thin man dressed casually in dark slacks, an open sport coat, and a cashmere sweater greets me when I dare face the killer. The coldest pair of eyes stare at me, piercing blue like a Caribbean sky on the left, dull grey like a battleship on the right. Those eyes lock on me, all business, ready to kill.

But his eyes are not what frighten me the most.

He allows me to see his light face, from his round chin to his shiny bald head, he allows me to look directly at him. That is what frightens me the most. He wears no mask, as if taking the time to conceal his murderous face is blasé. Despite the high-profile, jet-setting life I now live, I was raised in one of the roughest housing projects in Trenton, New Jersey. Donnelly Homes. My first love is one of the most feared men to ever walk the streets of New Jersey. I'd personally witnessed him dead a few dudes over the years. Each time he neglected to wear a mask, the only ones who left the room were the two of us.

This man wears no mask, so I know.

No witnesses.

As calm as an afterthought, the killer scoops Thomas from the floor and carries him to the window. He glances back at me, freezes me with his gaze, then peeks out at the traffic below. With no effort or remorse, he tosses Thomas's limp body over the rail.

I stifle an earth-shattering scream with my manicured hands.

He walks back over to me. Slowly. Methodically. He gives my naked body a once-over like I am chopped liver, like I'm not the chick men lust after all over the world. Women too. As if I am not the supermodel actress companies are throwing so many millions at, I can't even catch them with my insured hands and feet.

He looks at me like he's a professional.

For a brief moment in time our eyes lock. I attempt to elicit some empathy from him. Doesn't work. In a flash, he produces a stun gun and lights my ass up. I never see the prongs lash out, just feel jolts of electricity zipping through my body like an orgasm gone bad. He pulls the trigger ten times in as many seconds. My blood bubbles, my skin feels as if it is being melted away from my bones. The pain is unbearable. As I fight the battle of consciousness in the distant recesses of my mind, I finally hear screams rush up from the street below my window.

Then I black out.

***

Darkness. The highway groaning beneath me. Pipes grumbling under me. The strong scent of gasoline.

That is what awakens me.

I have no clue where I am or where I am going. All that matters to me is that I 'm still breathing. Unlike Thomas. I am in excruciating pain all over my body, severe, as if a toothache has spread to other parts of my body. But I am alive – and clothed, feels like a jogging suit, but I can't be sure. As I ride, I strive to gather enough wits and energy to mount an attack when an opportunity presents itself later.

Unfortunately, later comes sooner than I expect.

Later, I find that I am bound at the wrist and feet and gagged with a dirty sack crammed inside my mouth. Later, I realize I am not alone in the trunk. A putrid scent tells me this person is unaware of my presence. Later, the car grinds to a halt and I am face to face with a killer.

He snatches the trunk open, and I force my body to go stiffer than stone, praying that he believes I am unconscious. I peek through a half-closed eye and see a dusty shovel thrown carelessly over his shoulder. In the next instant, he reaches for me, and I cringe.

He chuckles. "Later for you likkle lady. Me 'ave special instructions for ya." His voice sounds like death multiplied. He carries a slight accent, maybe Caribbean, or even West African.

He yanks the dead body beside me from the trunk and drags it a few feet away from the car. We are in a wooded area, far off from civilization. I haven't heard this much silence in ages. Wildlife and shit howling, scurrying about. The smell of the wild descends upon me as I watch him walk out of view into the darkness. Seconds later, a deep thud echoes into the night, and a light cloud of dust billows my way. I hear the killer walking back toward me mumbling something about getting his clothes dirty.

The dust settles and he materializes before me, looming dark and scary. I begin to panic, frantically trying to loosen my reins, to no avail. He towers above me, peering down with a poker face. A light sheen of sweat frames his bald head, and musk rises from his body like steam. For too many uncomfortable seconds, he just stares at me.

"Wha' so make a maan wan kill woman this beautiful?" he whispers to himself, shaking his head. For a split second, I foolishly believe I have a chance. Then he shrugs his broad shoulders and says aloud, "Oh well, his choice."

He raises the sharp end of the shovel at my head.

Immediately, I think about Tiffany. Then, I see my whole life flash behind my eyes...

My childhood visits to my native Ethiopia before hard times crashed upon my family. The first day we moved to New Jersey. My homegirls from Donnelly Homes who I used to creep into Wilbur Section with to see boys. I see Menelik, my first, and only true, love. I see his dark eyes, curly hair, and enchanting smile. I see Italy, France, South Africa, Jamaica, and a host of other exotic locales I'd visited over the years. I see the Caribbean, with Menelik and without him. I see my first time having sex – with Menelik. I see my first time with a woman – with Menelik and without him. I see that fateful day when I left Menelik. Of all the things we participated in, sometimes gruesome acts, I'd never seen him cry until that day. I see my first fashion show, me strutting down the catwalk, Menelik beaming in the front row like a proud husband. I see a thousand moments in the blink of an eye. Bundles of money, decapitated heads, shootouts, courtroom drama, prison cells.

I see snapshots of my kaleidoscopic life in the blink of an eye.

Those snapshots simultaneously reveal to me that I am going to die, and who is responsible. My initial thought is that Slim's cronies from the SKG finally tracked me down, just as they had done Tiffany, however, my intuition tells me that it isn't Slim after all. My gut tells me exactly who has orchestrated this campaign of terror.

Menelik.

As much as I wanted to be in denial about it over the years, I knew that Menelik never released the sting of my betrayal. I had left him for dead so many years ago, and then sprinkled salt on the wound by hooking up with his brother. Then, in their world, I betrayed him too. I knew that neither one of those brothers would let that go. Regardless of how high I climbed the ladder to success, the hood will always consume me.

Suddenly, an eerie silence envelops me. Maybe it's the peace of the reaper coming to collect his due. I open my eyes to meet my killer just as he is driving a shovel toward my neck. I close my eyes and await the inevitable. I don't even scream.

But nothing happens.

I slowly open my eyes and see the killer with the shovel in mid-swing. He stops abruptly, tosses the shovel aside, and reaches into his pocket to retrieve a phone. The phone is buzzing like a hive of bees. On the sleek screen is my first love. The killer steps back from me, but I can still hear him as he barks into the phone.

"Yeah?" He cut his eyes at me and sighs. "Uh... well I ran into a little problem, but I took care of it. A two-for-one for you, I guess."

A professional. Just like I thought, Menelik had purchased a professional to take me out.

I can hear Menelik's voice ripping through the phone, then the killer's whole demeanor changes.

"Wait, say that again... no... but... but you paid me to bring you her head...it's not about the money. I gave you my word... uh-huh... uh-huh...okay. You got it."

The killer ends the call and stuffs the phone back into his pocket. He cracks a smile at me.

Then he zaps me with the stun gun until I no longer care.

CHAPTER 24

Menelik

I ease the G-Wagon down the long, muddy trail with my mind in a hazy cloud. My eyes are focused on the dirt road before me being illuminated by the bluish-tinted high beams, but my thoughts are a million miles away. More like one-hundred miles away, back in Trenton, New Jersey where this all started. I never thought it would come to this. I have become more than the man I ever thought I could be. A full-fledged multi-millionaire with a beautiful supermodel as a wife, homes in multiple continents, and not a care in the world.

Except one.

I trek down the winding path until I finally see the old Lincoln with the suicide doors sitting in a clearing. I hear the pipes rumbling before I even get to the car. I pull beside the Lincoln and scan the area before exiting. Once I'm sure the coast is clear, I grab my blade and pistol and hop out the truck.

"Hello, sir," the assassin greets me with a bit of concern. "Is everything okay?"

I ignore him and walk over to the back of the Lincoln. "Pop the trunk. I want to see her."

I step back and, with abated breath, I wait for him to open the trunk. Mere seconds feel like years as I wait to come face-to-face with my torrid past.

"She should be awake now," he mumbles as he stands beside me and points his key at the trunk. He presses a button, and the huge trunk slowly glides open to reveal Makeda bound and gagged.

"Here she is, all wrapped up in a pretty bow for you."

I see her face and freeze momentarily. Even bound and gagged, she is still beautiful. Her eyes flutter open, land on me, and then grow as big as dinner plates.

I stare at her in a mixture of resentment, desire, and rage. I close my eyes and flashes of our time together temporarily blind me. I recall how soft her lips are, how sweet her scent and taste used to feel on my tongue. I recall the times she held me down, driving away from the scenes of a crime with me, or sitting in silence as I recounted my dirty deeds. I recall her walking down the runway for the first time, me beaming a smile at her like a proud teacher. I recall it all in a matter of seconds.

I blink and recall the other side of those memories. I recall being sentenced to prison as I fell on a sword for her. I recall the moment Sophie told me that Makeda had moved on with her life. That empty feeling I felt that day resurface in my gut and almost buckle me. I recall seeing her walk into court on the news with my twin brother as I sat in a cell, sulking. I recall seeing my brother on visitation behind a glass awaiting his death date. The memories speed toward me like a locomotive finally reaching its destination.

"Pull her out," I order.

As the assassin snatches her up, she attempts to mumble through the gag but fails miserably. He drags her from the trunk and pitches her at my feet on the ground.

I look down at Makeda in a combination of disgust and pity. She peers up at me in total fear.

"Come on, let me see you work," I instruct the assassin. "You have rope?"

"I do."

"Good. String her up in that tree right there."

The assassin wastes no time. He wraps a thick rope around Makeda's neck and drags her over to a huge tree. Makeda kicks and chokes on her gag, but its useless. The assassin ties a metal object to the other side of the rope and tosses it over a thick branch. Then, he pulls down on the rope, slowly hoisting Makeda into the air...

***

Makeda

When the trunk opened, and I saw Menelik standing there, I felt a sense of relief. I thought he was coming to save me. Then, reality wakes me up and I find myself being dragged across the muddy ground with a rope around my neck.

I am too weak to put up a real fight, and I'm sure even if I want to put up a fight, it would've been futile. This is the end for me. I know it, and as I feel myself being hoisted high into the air, I accept my fate.

I stare at Menelik as I rise. I try to beam my thoughts to him, let him know that I am sorry for all the pain I caused him, let him know that despite it all, I still love him. On pure instinct, I attempt to escape the rope bound to my back, but it's futile. I look to the ground in defeat and swear I see a frown crease Menelik's brow. Just as quickly as it comes, it fades, replaced by a cruel smirk.

Suddenly, the rope begins to constrict tighter around my neck. I kick my legs flailing into the damp night air. I strain against the binds on mt wrist behind my back, but nothing gives. I am trapped, suspended high in the air by a rope, hanging on a tree like a slave in the Antebellum South. I attempt to scream, but my words come out in a hard wheeze instead. My breathing becomes short and ragged. I hold my breath, thinking that if I don't try to breath, then I can't lose my breath. Wrong.

The rope snatches tighter around my neck the more I resist, so I finally just release my will to the Creator. My head dangles on my chest allowing me to gaze at Menelik as he stares up at me with a blank face. Then, just as I struggle to inhale my final jagged breath, I see it.

A lone tear slides down Menelik's face. He mouths the words, *"I love you."*

Then, darkness envelopes me.

Menelik

A mixture of emotions consume me as I watch Makeda take her last breath, but the prevailing feeling is vindication. I realize that I still love her, but too much has been done in this life for that love to ever be anything more than a useless emotion. I note that even in death, she is still beautiful, but her betrayal has been too ugly of a sin to reward.

"Okay, that's that with that," I say to the assassin. "I want you to burn her body and make sure I get the ashes. Got it?"

"Yes sir."

I climb inside the G-Wagon. Only then do I allow my tears to flow freely as I watch him cut Makeda down from the tree. Her body lands with a thud. Moments later, he wraps her dead body in plastic and toss her back into the trunk of the Lincoln.

My phone shrills to life and snatches me back to reality. It's my wife. I gather my emotions and answer the call.

"Hi Beautiful."

"Hi handsome. I guess you won't make it back to the city in time."

"No, I won't."

"Menelik?"

"Yes?"

"I love you."

"I love you too."

"Oh, and Happy New Year!!!!!"